About the au

I believe I was born with a passion not for ice cream but for space.

As far as I remember myself, I kept looking at the sky with the intricate clouds looking like funny characters or sometimes jumping, roaring animals. In a moment the pictures would transform into something different but just as entertaining.

Even more, I was fascinated by the night sky, full of the flickering stars of our galaxy — The Milky Way — the moon and the deepest darkness of the cosmos.

It is our home isn't it? The beginning and the riddle of our lives are hidden there...

It gives endless opportunity to mankind for discoveries. Just be curious!

We had a quirky science teacher at school and we adored him. I am greatly thankful to the person who ignited my interest in science and laid the way for me to become a physicist.

I ended up working in a research centre after University and I loved each and every day of my job.

I hope the book will wake your imagination and shape your dreams on the way to discover more about our home — the Universe.

KINGDOM IN PERIL:
A CURIOUS FABLE

Lora Gridneva

KINGDOM IN PERIL
A CURIOUS FABLE

Vanguard Press

VANGUARD PAPERBACK

© Copyright 2020
Lora Gridneva

The right of Lora Gridneva to be identified as author of
this work has been asserted by her in accordance with the
Copyright, Designs and Patents Act 1988.

A CIP catalogue record for this title is
available from the British Library.

ISBN 978 1 78465 774 1

Vanguard Press is an imprint of
Pegasus Elliot MacKenzie Publishers Ltd.
www.pegasuspublishers.com

First Published in 2020

Vanguard Press
Sheraton House Castle Park
Cambridge England

Printed & Bound in Great Britain

ACKNOWLEDGMENTS

I would like to express my gratitude to:

The editor, Oliver Heathcote.

The graphic designer, Daria Belotsvetova for the covers of the book.

The scientist, Dr Nigel Evans, for providing stunning pictures of the Milky Way galaxy and, also for consulting on space facts.

The illustrator, Joe Davey.

PART ONE

Chapter 1

In a kingdom there lived rather strange, bizarre creatures. Even the king himself was wondering whence they had come to his state, and they were just becoming more and more numerous.

For example, there were the long, grey and scaly ones. They were no larger than an old child's shoe, but they were so unpleasant that, once having seen them, you'd try to avoid them as soon as you began to hear their characteristic scritchy-scratchy br-sh-shh noise which they produced by means of lots of twig-like side legs. They had heads too of course but not on their shoulders like all normal people; their heads were practically on the ground. Their eyes were looking all the time only down at the ground and all that they could see was just a dusty road along which they scratched in the morning to work at point 'A', and in the evening home to their favourite holes, point 'B'.

They were, it must be said, very industrious workers. They liked to sort out different documents with their numerous legs and lay them on different shelves so that, in the offices where they worked, order would reign. Their boss, an unusually large and fat gentleman in a grey scaly suit, liked to dominate these weak-willed grey centipedes. He

kept them in great poverty and unquestioning obedience. So the poor scalies often had to work for twenty hours a day, and many, who couldn't stand such hard work, withered and died.

But Mr Pot Belly didn't regret it for a minute, he just ordered the cleaner to sweep them away with a broom. However, the really hard workers were 'rewarded'; he'd send them rustling off to other offices to deliver the important documents.

And the documents could be really important; they described different events happening in the kingdom. For example, there was the interesting story about one poor Mr Skinny, whose pockets were so full of holes that they couldn't hold money, who couldn't' pay his rent to Mr Pot Belly. Pot Belly became very angry at the unfortunate pauper and out of spite began to shout wildly, showing his tonsils. In his rage he grew wider and wider and suddenly all the buttons on his new vest popped and flew off in different directions. Uh-oh, it was the last straw! So he came up with a nasty idea of how to laugh at poor Skinny. He couldn't get money out of him because of his extreme poverty so he decided to amuse himself with a joke, a cruel joke. He said Skinny would not have to repay his debt if he would cook for him every day and not dare to put a single crumb in his own mouth. "I'll set up cameras all round and they'll be watching you," he threatened.

There was nothing to be done so Skinny agreed. It should be noted here that he was a quick-witted man. He decided not to give the fat man healthy foods — like salads, vegetables and fruit, soup and milk, meat and fish. Instead he began to cook for Pot Belly all the things he loved — puddings and pies, pastries and ice cream — all in abundance and all were fattier and sweeter. He really liked mountains of rosy hot donuts with cream for breakfast, piles of greasy crispy chips and fried pies with Coca-Cola for lunch and finally for dinner there would be a basin of ice cream drizzled with chocolate. Mr Pot Belly's waistcoat was tighter with every meal and popped more and had already started splitting at the seams, but he did not realise the danger. He liked his sweet chocolate life.

But one hot summer morning, Skinny came to Pot Belly as usual to cook for his tormentor and, to his great joy, did not find him in his huge armchair. Not only was he not in the chair but generally nowhere to be seen! But on the ceiling and the walls there were fragments of his exploded vest, and Mr Fatty had disappeared, evaporated! He had burst like a balloon and there was not a shred of him left!

What a joy it was and there was so much happiness and fun around the house among the tenants who hated their paunchy landlord but were also afraid of him. And now they were rid of him!

They sprayed each other with bottles of Coca-Cola, flew kites in the air and threw balls of ice cream. Outdoors cheerful confusion reigned. People smiled, laughed and thanked their deliverer — such a brave and resourceful neighbour.

However, such successful endings were not common in the kingdom.

Chapter 2

Incidentally, these pot-bellied creatures caused concern not only to ordinary people but also, as mentioned, to the king. They didn't look at all as if they could possibly be proud of their appearance. Just imagine if you were a creature with a stomach like a huge pumpkin and with a head like a pencil! From constant anger the head tapered over time to resemble a sharpened pencil, and with constant greed the belly would swell and turn into a great big watermelon or pumpkin. As for legs, they were short and crooked, because they couldn't withstand the weight of the pumpkin belly!

These paunchy men were not as hard-working as the 'grey scaly' ones, not at all. They all strove to catch the poor and unfortunate losers in their network and torment them — because they had no other interest in life.

Of course, the king did not at all like this stratum of the population in his illustrious kingdom. What would the foreign ambassadors say when they saw these strange creatures? Neither man nor beast! Freaks in fact! The king was upset and worried, and decided to convene the council of elders and together come up with what on earth to do about them.

They thought hard, wondering and scratching their heads, and finally decided to send the king to God. God knows everything and tells you what to do. He began to collect himself. The way was not easy, and also technically extremely complicated. After all, the king would have to turn from being a normal person into God's visitor. Aha, now I will talk about this complex, this most complex procedure.

The procedure for this was that the king would have to go through two stages of transformation in order to converse with God in his godly language. It's a matter of courtesy to speak the language of the country you visit, and the king was a most polite man.

In the first stage, the king — with the help of sophisticated scientific equipment — would be transformed into an energy cloud. This is a cloud that could jump up and run and gallop, and even fly like a kite. The only thing that it could not do was think, and reason, and talk. So, in a second step, other smart machines would teach this royal cloud all the tricks of our very complex brain: well, like to write, and see and hear and solve challenging puzzles, and even to feel sad and laugh. The result would be that the king would appear very beautiful, shining with all the colours of the rainbow. In particular the principal colours would suit his majesty — red, like a raging fire, green like grass and trees, and blue like our blue sky and azure ocean or sea.

And so, arrayed like this, the king would be absolutely ready to fly to meet God. Oh, what miracles can science and technologies create!

Finally came the day when the king was going to fly to God. It was a sunny summer day and there was not a cloud in the sky. The entire king's entourage and the people of the kingdom came to see how he would fly to God. The king himself was worried since he was doing it for the first time. It's no joke to say 'fly above the sky' into the realm of God! However, the king kept a straight face and gave not a hint that he was shaking with fright.

He entered the vehicle of reincarnation, and everyone waited with bated breath for what would happen next; what would their king turn into? Ticking hearts beat seconds, time dragged incredibly slowly, as it always does, bothersome when one is really waiting for something...

But we have to be patient, and it's not easy. So the children of the kingdom are taught this ability at school; well, that's exactly how to write or read. So all behaved well. An hour passed, and suddenly everybody saw the iridescent cloud fly out from the semicircular roof of the reincarnation car and ascend into the blue sky. It was an indescribably beautiful sight! Just imagine, a bright, blue sky, and carried up in the twisting sparkling iridescent cloud — the king! It became smaller and smaller, and soon turned into a tiny, shimmering asterisk.

All was done! The king was in heaven!

The people, excited by the launch of the king through space to God, were in no hurry to leave. All the options were discussed: what would happen to the king, would he meet with God, and would God suggest to him what to do with these noxious, unpleasant creatures? Is it possible they will return to their original appearance and friendly character? In general, there was a lot of wild guessing and fevered speculation. Just after midnight the people began to disperse to their homes, awaiting news from the sky in the near future.

Chapter 3

But now we have to tell how our brave king got to God, and how it was unique in the history of mankind — this meeting between God and man. The king was in fact incomparably brave and all because he genuinely cared about his people and the friendliness in his kingdom. His desire to solve the problem gave him unprecedented courage.

Well, the king travelled without, it could be said, particular obstacles. Congestion in space had not yet developed. It was just that the tail of his cloud had been pierced and scattered in the dust by a piece of some old disintegrated rocket. However, as a cloud, he didn't feel any pain and hoped that God would correct his cloud's deformed tail. But who knows how this loss would affect his appearance when he again took human form? Maybe this clash would deprive him of his legs? Or one leg? In short, it would be necessary to bring his cloudy manifestation into full working order. But that was not the point. What the king was most concerned about was finding God and how he would communicate with him. Everything, everything was unknown to him, and unseen. It was scary!

However, he worried needlessly. God himself found him and called. And what was most surprising of all — the king now had neither eyes nor ears but he somehow felt in some supernatural way that God was calling him and he knew which way his magisterial cloud needed to move. Then, more and more surprising and amazing, the king felt the moment when he appeared before God, and he began to speak with him.

As we already know, the cloud king had no face or mouth, and he certainly couldn't speak. Oh no! But he talked with God! Mentally. God asked him questions, which appeared suddenly in his cloudy head, and the king sent back the answers with the help of his thoughts. The king felt excited by the wonderful communion with God and at the same time he felt himself embraced by heavenly peace and tranquillity. It seemed now to him that all the problems of his kingdom would in some miraculous way be resolved and dispersed.

He felt that in God's abode, with all its cloudiness, he sensed a boundless space filled with myriads of lightning-fast fireflies that emitted short bursts of some multi-coloured magical, kindly light. There was a pleasing sensation of the gentle glowing of all God's realm.

These fireflies were omniscient God's helpers. Each of them was like the ears and the eyes of God. They knew everything that was happening on Earth, in any of it, even in very remote areas. They knew everything about every person on Earth. Nothing and no one could hide from their lightning-speed appearance. They were reporting to God about everything that happened in the countries or in homes or at schools — who fought with someone and who made friends with someone. This is why God is called 'omnipresent'.

God would think hard and then take the wisest decision — whom to punish and whom to pardon and reward. And so was arranged the God-sphere, the all-seeing, all-knowing, all-understanding, an expanse of sky which we humans cannot see or feel, but if we want to talk to God and we focus, then he will certainly hear us, because he has a myriad of ear-fireflies.

So the king expressed his concern in his thoughts at what strange creatures had appeared in his kingdom, and that he did not know what to do with them. He sent these thoughts to God. God replied that he had heard about them — the fireflies had told him everything — and that he still pondered what to do. You, please, do not think that God can easily resolve absolutely all the problems in the world; some of them come to the point of such confusion and complexity that even God has to think and to think very hard what decision to take.

Now he proposed to the king to go to the star, Prima, home of the superbiotechs. Their civilisation is much older than that on Earth and is one of the most advanced among the neighbouring galaxies. God advised the king to invite the group of superbiotechs to Earth, and they would try to help the king.

Chapter 4

The path to the star, Prima, was not a short one as well as being highly dangerous. It was impossible to avoid crossing a hostile neighbouring Antipodal galaxy. Aggressive inhabitants of some stars of this galaxy could even be sent in pursuit of the spaceship and capture the king as a prisoner. Then he would not escape 'scientific analysis', when His Royal Highness would be subjected to all sorts of surgical dissections and mental tests, after which the king, as such, would have ceased to exist.

The hostile galaxy needed to examine a person better, to find his weaknesses in order to find ways to defeat humanity. It wanted to grab for itself more and more planets. Its greed knew no bounds. It was the highest and most 'laudable' trait of their character; and the most greedy, super-greedy Antipodal of the year was awarded a medal at the annual celebration for the most insatiable greed, and a few bags of disgustingly smelly bugs, which he then was happy to count and recount until he had eaten all of them.

However, if the king passed unnoticed by the Antipodals' galaxy during the flight, then he would have a chance to introduce himself to superbiotechs and discuss the terms and conditions of helping the Earth. Superbiotechs were way ahead in their technical and biological development compared with people on Earth. Surely, they would restore human faces and friendly natures to these poor creatures on Earth — thus hoped the king.

The king found out from God that his people had been infected by viruses which had been brought from the hostile galaxy. And only superbiotechs could help remove these virus-parasites from infected bodies and minds. They were ve-ee-ery clever!

The viruses thrived on the good, kind and tasty energy of a human being, draining it and turning it into a terrible individual: first children and people would forget how to smile and laugh, then much worse, they would become a thief, bully, cheat or glutton. In addition, they could change the look of a human being beyond recognition and convert it into a monster or something funny.

The Antipodals hoped to conquer the planet Earth. In fact, after infection of a human being by the virus, he would become a 'good for nothing'. Or he or she could turn out to be without any will power and do whatever they were ordered to do — for example, swear or fight people, become terribly lazy and not want to work or study, or would hurt children and animals — and oh, so many more different misfortunes. Here, maybe you can add something else, huh? Come on, think about it, my friend...

Well, let's see now, what the king decided? Whether he should fly to the star Prima or whether his own life was more valuable and the travelling wasn't worth the risk?

Chapter 5

The king has been deep in thought. He deliberated: "To fly means to jeopardise my life, only one life, but not to fly means that slowly but surely all my people will perish. The viruses would multiply and affect more and more people." He sighed heavily. "Uh-uh ...well, shall I hope for the best but be prepared for anything?" whispered the king and decided to fly. He loved his people and was ready to do everything in his power for them. The king sent his thought to God about his decision. God approved it and added that it would help him in his difficult journey with the assistance of the ubiquitous myriad fireflies. "You deserve my help," said God "because you are a brave and good man. However, you yourself must be prepared for a variety of difficult tests on this flight. The Antipodal galaxy is governed by hostile forces. Its goal is to capture us — the bright galaxies — and set up darkness, unhappiness and violence throughout the universe.

"This war between light and darkness has lasted for a long time, millions of years, and nobody knows when it will end. But we must not give even an inch; otherwise the whole world will plunge into complete everlasting darkness. We serve the light for good and live for the sake of the world.

"I'll give you one of my stellar spaceships. It's invisible. As you have probably realised, here in space man does not need eyes. They are only on Earth to help you to see things, but here everything happens at the wave level, and according to the laws of gravity. It is hard to understand this now that the eyes are not needed, and you cannot touch or feel a thing! Your civilisation is very young, and you have not yet discovered many laws of the universe. You have a long and interesting path ahead in science. Well, now, just believe everything that I say. God has finished. I wish you, the people, only good and kind things in your life."

Then he added, "As soon as you place yourself in my ship and think that you need to be on the star, Prima, you will soon find yourself there. Your thoughts will have my strength and power and will be transmitted over distance almost instantaneously — you need only to think and make a decision.

"In highly developed civilisations, subjects inhabiting stellar worlds understand the complex language of waves. They learn to understand it in school exactly like you learn your alphabet. 'And what do they look like?' you'd ask. Ooh, you would never guess! No bulging eyes, or elephant's trunk, or terrible drooling dragons. No, they are energy subjects called 'ensubs', and they are invisible. Ensubs are like blobs of energy and have an energy shape. Yes, they are not visible but you may simply feel them like you can feel heat or cold. You don't see faces and figures of heat or cold, but you sense them. Also, you will feel them and even understand what the subjects want.

"They will send you wave signals, and your brain will take them and decode them and translate these signals into human language. That's it, my dear king." God made a little pause and then continued, "My firefly will show you the Interstellar Ship. Get ready for the flight, Your Majesty, and when you need my help, just imagine Me in front of you, and I will be with you immediately."

Chapter 6

"That's the story," thought the king. He still could not get over all that had happened to him. He somehow prepared himself to meet God, but really was not yet ready for a further journey to the star Prima now, and then all this wave transformation. "Oh, it's all too hard for an ordinary person to understand the laws of the cosmos."

He was a king, and not a scientist. "Yes, in my realm people make a lot of successful attempts to master communication at the wave level," thought the king. "Of course, we have radio, television, radar, Internet, mobile phone and so on, but the advanced subjects communicate directly, bypassing all this technical equipment and gadgets! They can read each other's thoughts and even create the image before your eyes! They can do so much that none of our wild fantasies can imagine all that they can do! Oh, my white old head," the king kept exclaiming, rocking from side to side. "But I have to, I have to do it for the sake of my people."

Here are the adventures our king ventured to do. What do you think: will our brave king survive? Let us call him Smelan, — yes, king Smelan, which means brave.

Chapter 7

Smelan sent to God his message that he was quite ready to fly to the star Prima. Almost immediately, he found his 'cloudy' Majesty in the star ship, and only when he thought he'd got comfortable and even liked the cockpit and his bedroom, did he suddenly begin to notice that his cloudy body had started to change. He suddenly felt that he was losing lightness. The cloudiness began to thicken, and even some silhouettes began to take shape... "My goodness, here are my hands and feet, and... my head! Oh, all my body is back! What's happening?" the king marvelled.

Suddenly he heard in his head God's voice, "Don't worry about anything. It's necessary that you have your natural body appearance. When you arrive at the star Prima, they have to see what a human being looks like and then they will make all the required tests to know everything about people so that if they come to Earth then this knowledge will help them to act quickly and efficiently. In order to do all the tests, they will put you into a deep sleep and freeze your body so you will feel no pain, you'll feel nothing. Now don't be so anxious, after their investigation they will restore your body and appearance to exactly as it was. Superbiotechs are kind and humane; they are totally opposite to the Antipodals."

Smelan calmed down and decided to completely surrender to the will of God, for He is our God who knows everything and He is good." Now the king had to work with his mind and send into space a very powerful idea:

1. "I, King Smelan, go to the star Prima.

2. The hostile Antipodal galaxy does not notice my Interstellar Spaceship. I successfully complete my flight.

3. I will be greeted on Prima by friendly superbiotechs."

Such a set of commands the king mentally sent into space. He closed his eyes and braced himself for a miracle, and more miracles.

Chapter 8

It took a few minutes but maybe a few hours, according to the king he didn't know. He was lost in the terms of time in the cosmos. Suddenly the king felt as though millions of needles pierced his body, and as though they sucked the power out of him. It happened so fast that he barely had time to send a distress call to God — SOS. Here Smelan grasped that his ship had been attacked by Antipodals: it meant he had not concentrated enough, and his notion of 'pass the galaxy unnoticed by Antipodals' was weak. That's why they discovered him, and attacked. The king felt he was losing consciousness.

However, God managed to get the distress signal from the royal traveller and promptly dispatched fireflies to the rescue. Fireflies at top speed raced after the ship.

Soon they caught up with it and began to neutralise the Antipodals and cleanse them from the ship. This did not turn out to be easy. The Antipodals brought into play the latest scientific achievements of the galaxy. They learned how to quickly change the appearance of their own energy, taking on the configuration of the fireflies and in the ensuing confusion it was not so easy to detect and neutralise them. A large group of fireflies had been affected; they lost their orientation in the wave field but hoped that when they returned home to their galaxy, they would be able to repair these serious defects.

Still, good deeds, as we know, win through at the end of the day. The fireflies managed to neutralise millions of Antipodals and clear them from the ship. Now they had to leave the Interstellar ship before landing on Prima and return to the sphere of God. On the star Prima the electromagnetic environment and extremely high temperatures — several hundred degrees! — were inappropriate for them. They wouldn't be able to survive for even a minute and would vaporise instantly.

Chapter 9

Our Smelan meanwhile remained senseless and paralysed. Here in this state he appeared before the superbiotechs when the Interstellar ship landed under control of the auto-robot.

Although the king was senseless, his eyes were now open, and he could see and even think and analyse. He realised that he was attacked by antipodals during the flight, which made him writhe in unbearable pain and then fireflies came to help him. Also, he realised that while he was completely unconscious, the Interstellar Ship landed on the star Prima.

Soon Smelan sensed rather than saw that something was happening around him. He recollected that God had told him that the star worlds are inhabited by ensubs, and that they are invisible to a human being. Smelan thought that they were there, beside him. Suddenly, as if to prove his conjecture, he began to feel he could move his fingers and toes, and this was the beginning of his full recovery. Soon he was able to freely bend, unbend and smile, but he wanted to laugh too, because he was so happy that all the horrors of his journey lay behind him. He was among friends (palpable even though invisible).

Now, the king had to decide how he would tell inhabitants of Prima about the problem that arose in his kingdom, and ask them to visit Earth. He still did not see anyone and, of course, didn't know the language in which he could talk to superbiotechs. The king still remained deep in thought when suddenly he saw a hologram movie that hung near him, at eye level. Smelan saw himself -- and everything about what he had just thought — in pictures. Without words and language, everything was clear — as if it was a story in pictures.

He was absolutely amazed and delighted at the same time. Now King Smelan knew that everything he would think about his new friends would be perceived at the energy level as each thought is an energy pulse. It always happens like this: as soon as you think about something good or bad, right away in all directions flow energy waves, good or bad. That's how incredibly interesting we are. So, my friend, try your best to think positive and about good things.

So, Smelan decided to focus his thoughts and send them as short and clear messages, to make the superbiotechs understand the situation on Earth.

Letter One:

On the planet Earth in the solar system viruses were discovered. They originated from a hostile Antipodal galaxy. Viruses infect humans and turn them into evil, aggressive and cruel monsters, or into helpless and mindless creatures."

Letter Two:

People cannot cope on their own with these viruses and the population becomes infected very fast. Humankind on Earth will perish and hostile forces will overwhelm Earth if we do not get help."

Letter Three:

"God thinks that only you, superbiotechs, are able to help us and to eliminate the terrible viruses on Earth which are destroying people."

Letter Four:

"I, as Earth's representative, appeal to you with a huge request for assistance. Please, consider the possible options for help and I'll take them whatever your conditions."

Letter Five:

"I hope for a positive response and all Earthlings thank you in advance. They await my return with great hope."

Thus, Smelan wrote all these letters in his mind and started one after the other slowly and, concentrating as much as possible, to transmit them out of his head. He noted to himself that he didn't feel tired at all, as if his whole body got some sort of energy from the outside that he had not seen, but sensed. He felt a surge of strength and vigour and in high spirits despite all that he had so recently endured, as if someone helped him to forget it all quickly and switch to the present moment.

Chapter 10

While Smelan was waiting for an answer, he had some time to look around. However, he saw nothing fantastic. He felt that he was in some isolated space and as though comfortably suspended in a gentle and fluffy cloud. Visibility was there but, as it were, at the same time it was not. The eye could not determine the boundary where an air cloud started and where it ended.

Some little time had passed as it seemed to him, and suddenly Smelan saw a picture appearing from the cloud. The picture showed letters flying forwards and backwards and it was a clear message inviting the king to communicate.

Smelan said, "Yes, of course," in his mind. He then saw a series of pictures showing a process of learning with a lot of question marks. Symbols used in the pictures were clear to understand and for the king it looked like an interesting game. He figured out that Primlean superbiotechs were not only learning about the Earthlings but also learning their language. He smiled, he was very happy to feel that communication was going well and maybe soon Primleans would be able to talk to him in a human voice.

He was then offered a choice of images with which the king would feel comfortable to talk. Superbiotechs can take on any image and appear in any form, but they wanted the king to choose the picture as the image before his eyes with which he would be happy to talk.

The king thought and thought and chose a green lawn with a mighty oak on it spreading its branches across. The green lawn was pleasing to the eyes and reminiscent of his native land, and a strong oak felt as if he was sending out powerful energy and confidence. The superbiotech did not delay a minute, and the lawn and the oak appeared in the cloud space.

Then Smelan heard a voice that sounded as if it came from this same green lawn. "Wow, that was fast!" a thought flashed, "actually incredibly fast to learn a language in minutes! I never knew somebody in my kingdom with the same head-spinning ability. I'd better prepare myself for all sorts of things like this."

The voice explained to him that the superbiotechs were going to turn off his mind, well, as it were, to freeze it, to make the necessary tests of humankind. There was nothing to be afraid of as the return to the normal state would take place painlessly; he would feel as if he had slept a little. Afterwards the superbiotechs would show him their star. They would make for him a special Prima-suit. After having all tests done they would know what kind of suit needed to be made, and what the human body would need to be protected on the star Prima. The king listened to everything and decided to trust them implicitly, as he felt he had met very good and kind friends.

King Smelan didn't notice how he fell into oblivion, and how he came to himself again. He really had the feeling of having had a little nap, and now felt well rested and refreshed. He heard nice starry music and slowly in the cloud a hologram began to appear, something vague and it was difficult to make out what it was. "Ah, this is my cloudy head; there are no clear thoughts in it now, and this is reflected exactly on the milky screen. So, I need to put my thoughts in order:

"Firstly, I have to tell my friends that I feel fine; secondly, it is necessary for me to find out how the tests went; thirdly, to ask about a tour of the star."

Hardly had he formulated these clear thoughts in his mind than on the screen appeared a green meadow with wild flowers and a mighty oak in the centre; ah, well, just the view from his window in the palace! The mood jumped from good to excellent. "So," thought Smelan, "what's going to happen next?" Then he heard a pleasant voice, as though it was the familiar voice of one of his friends but he couldn't remember whose? It was not so important now.

The voice said that the superbiotechs were very pleased that he felt good after the tests were run. In answer to Smelan's second question, they said that the tests went well, and they now had a full bioenergetic image of the human form. Now they would be able to help Earthlings and recover any distortion of the human body by viruses. The king was literally beside himself with happiness. He could barely control himself. As you all know, of course, self-control — control of your emotions — is one of the most important qualities of any royal person, and which all of us would do well to learn.

Well, then, the king wanted to jump up to the ceiling, to laugh as much as ten people, and even — you'll of course forgive the king — to jump on one leg and hum the tune: Taa-ta-taaaam; lyaa-Laa-lyaaa! With difficulty he could still refrain from this adorable 'nonsense', but a happy smile never left his face.

Chapter 11

The following day was to be a tour of the star. The superbiotech told him that his suit was ready, which they had specially manufactured for the first human guest on Prima. Their star is different from Earth in all possible ways: for example, the star does not have atmosphere or water; there are no green lawns and flowers, not even trees, animals and blue ocean. "It is difficult to list all that is not here, but it's better if you, Your Majesty, will wear a spacesuit and we go on a tour; you will see everything with your own eyes," added a pleasant voice from the screen.

The hologram appeared to melt away in space and the king suddenly saw the suit, which was, as it were, floated towards him. Smelan began without delay to put on the suit. Someone helped him to cope with all the buckles, tubes, cylinders, sensors, and finally put on a helmet across which ran tracks of colour signals.

Now, our king really was ready to go on the tour. As soon as he thought about it, he saw that the cloud space around him cleared up, and instead the outlines of red and purple rocks began to emerge. It was not our blue or dark blue sky but instead black, like the night sky on Earth. In the black space orbited a hundred or two (one couldn't count them all at once) natural satellites — well,

46

just like our moon. Moreover, they were of different sizes and different colours. You cannot imagine so many breathtaking and unusually bright 'beauties', shining and flickering in the sky. Besides, they not only moved at different speeds, but also in different directions. The king felt dizzy from the unprecedented spectacle. "Oo-h! I think I'd better look down. Perhaps I should take a little break from this wonderful, magical whirling," whispered the king to himself.

However, when Smelan looked down on the rocks, over which he was flying slowly, he came to an even greater surprise. Yes, he saw no rivers, no green forests, no fields and seas, but saw the unusual colours of the rocks. They were a dark copper-red; they were also purple — the colour of magnesium — and dark gold. But the mystery of their soft glow, as it was iridescent and constantly changing, soon became clear to the king.

The rocks were wonderfully polished and different facets reflected the numerous moons that circled in the black sky. Well, just as our moon reflects in the water and the water becomes tinted silver. The spectacle of the cliffs was absolutely fantastic, fascinating, and you would want to watch and watch all that swirling and shimmering colour and the feeling as though you were seeing a wonderful magical dream as a child.

In short, this star with glowing moons moving on the black sky and reflecting the light from its intricate rock formations, led the king to total delight. His mind refused to believe his eyes. He felt totally exhausted by the abundance of these fantastic visions. And then he heard a soft and pleasant voice. Invisible, but accompanying him on his journey, the superbiotech offered him a rest.

He said that perhaps for the king this was enough impressions for the first time, and that now it would send him a dream. They would meet again when the king had had a rest. The suit adopted a horizontal position and quiet soothing music was heard. Smelan even fancied there was the gentle smell of forest violets but maybe this fragrance spread through the suit, only the king could not distinguish reality from illusion. He sank into oblivion, he fell asleep.

Chapter 12

Smelan awoke to what felt like a ray of sunlight that slid down his cheek and continued slowly with gentle warmth to move across his face. He opened his eyes and it took him a moment to remember where he was. However, instead of the black sky that so struck him the day before, he saw dazzlingly bright silvery and gold rocks — absolutely nothing like yesterday's landscape.

The suit slowly took on a vertical position, and again the same pleasant voice told him that they were diametrically opposite the pole of the star. "The star, like Earth, has two poles and they are very different from each other in rock formation," continued the superbiotech. At the North Pole the rocks are composed mainly of copper, magnesium and iron. Therefore, they reflect tones such as reddish, purple, and dark yellow. In this hemisphere of the star the sky is always black, and only the moons shining provide a colourful, magical lighting.

"Now we are in the southern hemisphere, at the South Pole. The southern hemisphere of our star is always drawn to the bright side of the twin stars. The rock species consist mainly of diamonds, sapphires and rubies, and so at this point there is always a dazzling iridescent glow of reflected radiation. In addition, we charge ourselves here, i.e. we 'eat' energy radiated by the rocks. The Ruling Committee of our star is also here. It ensures the coordination of all scientific centres and is aware of everything that happens on the star.

"Soon I'll introduce you to our Ruling Committee. Before that, I'll tell you a little about us, superbiotechs, how we operate and how we differ from people."

Chapter 13

The king got ready to listen. What was amazing was that, in all this time staying on the star, he never ate, and no one offered him so much as a crust of bread. But no, he just wasn't hungry. It was so surprising that he decided to ask the question mentally. Immediately he got the answer!

The superbiotech told him that on Earth we eat in order to obtain from the food calories, energy. Our body expends much effort to eat food, digest it, and extract from it the necessary energy. In addition, we must also expend a lot of effort to produce this food — grow fresh vegetables, fruits, grain for bread, corn, livestock for milk and cheese and all sorts of delicious yogurt, and then build plants and factories and bakeries that pack and prepare our food in the best possible way for the shelves of supermarkets. It is also necessary to earn money to buy whatever we want. In general, as it turns out, for most people for their whole life they just do what they need to earn their food to get energy to walk, talk, work, raise children, and so on.

This stage of evolution is ancient history for superbiotechs. They don't have tummies, or intestines, or bottoms — they don't need all of those any more. They learned how to provide themselves with energy without this complicated biological process — with a shortcut. When they need some energy, they charge themselves from very powerful charging points.

"Well," the Primlean continued, "I told you a little bit about superbiotechs and now I'll tell you a bit about our star. We Primleans certainly love our homeland — it is indescribably beautiful; you, Your Majesty, saw it yourself. However, in this era we are experiencing the greatest disappointment (in general we superbiotechs are not subject to the emotions), but this is a special, global event, and we are all in a state of serious concern.

"Our beautiful star is dying. She has lived a good stellar life — ten billion years — and now comes the time for her magic show to die. After all, you know, my friend, that stars die beautifully, and at the end of their lives they go quickly through various stages, from the 'red giant' stage to the 'white dwarf'. Each period in the life of a star is very beautiful. So, now our star is in the stage of synthesising heavy elements. The star is rapidly shrinking, and as it shrinks, it cools down and forms on the surface crystals of precious stones and minerals of various metals of unprecedented beauty. They are very small, but still very hot and therefore shine and sparkle and also reflect the light of our many satellites. Copper-magnesium-iron formations in the northern hemisphere, which cast a reddish-violet light, and diamond-sapphire crystal rocks interspersed with significant gold and silver in the southern hemisphere. The temperature of the star began to fall and now stands at just a few hundred degrees, but for you people it is still a very high temperature and you could not survive a few seconds — you would burn quicker than a match.

Now I invite you to relax again after all you've seen and heard during our excursions. I see from the state of your brain that you, Your Majesty, have received extremely rich information about our star and you are very excited. After a while you will calm down and then we will meet with the Governor of the Central Committee of the star.

"The Committee will propose a plan for the salvation of Earthlings and Earth from capture by the Antipodals. Our mission in the universe is to serve as a bright beginning, to disseminate ideas of goodness and progress, only because it makes your life worthwhile and enjoyable. But the Antipodals' galaxy aims to destroy the glow of life wherever they can extend their deadening reach. That is its nature, and in the universe of billions of years, there is a struggle beginning between light and dark. We must not stop in our quest to bring the joy of life and progress; otherwise eternal darkness will engulf all life in the universe."

These were the last words that the king heard and understood, then his mind was turned off and he fell into a pleasant dream.

Chapter 14

He dreamed of the Earth... His laughing, rosy-cheeked beautiful daughter, the princess, and his kingdom... his adorable wife and many friends and advisers... the blue ocean and rivers, and green meadows with cows and lambs... fertile fields and orchards.

It was also a vision of him and of those miserable creatures who were his subjects, transformed by wickedness into freaks. This dream was like a quilt — multi-coloured, consisting of separate pieces, but overall turned out completed as a whole quilt — as often happens in a dream: the picture of the whole kingdom. The dream was like guidance and prepared his thoughts and feelings for the meeting with the star Committee.

The king opened his eyes, still feeling in the power of the dream. He stretched with pleasure and thought of a cup of coffee. But he remembered where he was and it just made his mouth water. However, from nowhere appeared a silver tray and on it a cup of steaming coffee. The king thought he was still asleep, but decided to sip it, so irresistible was the aroma, and for a long time he didn't try it. The taste turned out to be excellent, well quite simply as good as the best coffee he had ever drunk in the kingdom. The king closed his eyes in pleasure. Blinked, blinked, and pinched himself.

"No, I am not asleep;" — the thought flashed through his mind — "oh, the wonders are still going on, playing with my mind on this amazing star, and these marvels I cannot explain!" But he remembered that he would be meeting with the star Committee. "Well, I am ready," the king thought to himself.

Chapter 15

After a while, the king began to distinguish the outline of the holographic image in the air, which he had requested so as to feel more confident during the conversation with the Committee. There was the green lawn and sturdy half-century-old oak of his garden. Smelan was a little nervous because of the complete unknown, but the sight of his native land and the images of the dream gave him peace of mind, clarity of thought and firmness.

His lawn with the oak moved slightly to the left and to the right appeared another hologram in which he saw, as if in the movies, the sparkling diamond cliffs of the southern hemisphere where he was now located.

"The Committee of Prima welcomes you, King Smelan. (He received the message in his brain.) "We were notified of the reasons for your visit, and that you need our help. Now again we perceive your thoughts, read the signals in your brain, and assure you that we can help you; we want to help you and do it with joy." The king received all these messages.

Smelan was beside himself with joy and tried to concentrate and express his gratitude by sending the committee a powerful, bright thought. The rocks changed colour after the sending by the king of his gratitude, and shimmered now in a delicate greenish-pink glow. "Aha, my thanks have reached them," thought the king. Then he heard the voice, coming as though from the rocks: "Dear Smelan, we need now to discuss the situation on Earth, and the possible options for saving the people and helping Earth. I am a historian and now interpreter; I shall take part in this communication with you. I learned the language of earthlings and in the last two days I have been mastering it. May I introduce myself — my name is Nuri."

The strange rocky voice continued: "The fact is there is an infection of Earthlings by viruses — this is the first but we are sure not the last attempt by the hostile galaxy to conquer Earth. In the study of your biological status and your DNA, we found some evolutionary weaknesses in your species. These include imperfections in your way of thinking.

"It will take thousands of years, for your way of thinking to develop and be close to perfection. You humans must go through this evolutionary path, as happened to our civilisation as we superbiotechs passed through it. But now you need help, as you have been discovered by the Antipodals who want to capture your civilisation.

"The imperfection of your mind is that sometimes you find it very hard to resist temptation, and often you people are seized with excessive selfishness, when you do not want to love anyone more than yourself. There is also for many people an overwhelming desire to taste all sorts of dubious and dangerous pleasures which first lure a person and then destroy and kill him. Besides, very often you are suffering from lack of will-power and you indulge yourselves in abundance with so many things which are actually very harmful for your physical and mental health; it means you can be very greedy — greedy for money, greedy for food, greedy for pleasure, and so on...

"It is here, on these weaknesses, that the Antipodals build their attack on Earthlings. They launch viruses, which increase your weaknesses tenfold, make them excessive, and when you find yourself facing a choice between doing something bad (you always know when you do bad) or refraining from a bad step, these viruses do not leave you in any doubt. As though bewitched, you take the worst possible solution. You then find yourself a victim of the mental destruction of your mind. This is the most sophisticated, devious and quickest of the ways to the conquest and enslavement of civilisations."

There was a pause. The Star Committee gave Smelan time to think about what he had heard. "So," continued the rocky voice, "we can restore the psyche and consciousness of the people who were struck by the Antipodal viruses. We can also create for each inhabitant of your kingdom a protective energy shell which the virus will not be able to penetrate and affect the consciousness. However, the population will be growing, children will be born. When we fly away, these children will be defenceless again and the viruses can again attack them.

The Star Committee was thinking about how to provide the residents of the kingdom with permanent protection from Antipodal attack. Newborn children could receive from superbiotechs a protective energy shell, well, just as they get vaccinated now against various serious diseases.

"To do this requires fulfilling two conditions:

"1. Your consent to having superbiotechs' presence on Earth. They would exist in a parallel world and would be invisible to all of you. They would communicate only with those Earthlings who are involved in the project.

"2. It is necessary, of course, to have the consent of the group of superbiotechs willing to go to Earth and ready to execute this mission. The consciousness of superbiotechs is free from selfishness and they always help when necessary.

"However, it would be a very long journey and a long stay possibly until the end of their life, in another galaxy in isolation from friends and family and their homeland — the star Prima. We cannot compel our Primleans and forcibly send them to Earth. Therefore, we will survey all the population of the star and see how many of us are willing to leave Prima and agree to fight the dark hostile forces. "Now, we give you time to think about everything that you've heard. We also need some time to poll the population. Relax, Your Majesty, we will soon meet again."

The pictures hanging in the air, as it were, faded.

Chapter 16

It didn't take Smelan long to think. The possibility of protecting the population of the kingdom from the attacks of the Antipodals, and not only living people but also future children, seemed to him magnificent, or even better — perfect. "My God, my God, that was good advice you gave me! Now, all these poor freaks will disappear! They will return to their human form and friendly disposition, and we all in the kingdom will live calmly and with dignity. People will feel a lot of joy, and fear and injustice will disappear."

The king was exultant. "Moreover, you could always rely on the benevolent advice of such true friends, the superbiotechs. After all, they would always be in a parallel world, unseen and unheard, but always ready to help. This is the best, most perfect solution for Earth and Earthlings!" the king rejoiced to himself.

However, after a while, when his excitement had died down somewhat, Smelan pondered whether he had the right to request such a huge favour. After all Primleans would have to leave their star, their homeland — so unusual and so beautiful — forever, maybe even for the rest of their lives, as the committee had said. "Oh, my poor head, again a difficult task! What should I do, how to resolve this quandary?"

The king didn't know how much time he spent in agonising meditations — maybe hours in Earth time, or maybe two weeks. The sense of time, like the sense of hunger, was for Smelan a forgotten concept. Here, in any case, they had no meaning.

His lengthy thoughts were suddenly interrupted by a voice:

"Calm down, Smelan, we have found a better solution. It is Nuri speaking and I would like to tell you the news. Superbiotechs do not necessarily need to be on Earth to monitor and ensure the protective shell of each infant. We will be able to create a protective field around the whole Earth. Then no malicious and destructive viruses will ever be able to infiltrate your atmosphere or people. We will create a machine that orbits Earth, in other words an artificial Earth satellite, which will provide a permanent bioenergetic protective field. We already have several projects with such a device. It will serve a million years and will then need to be replaced."

"We will meet again in a million years." (The superbiotech was joking, or maybe not... In fact. the king didn't know how long they live.) In the meantime, we have already started equipping the expedition and preparing to fly to Earth. Much to our surprise, it turns out that many superbiotechs would like to fly to Earth. This project, for saving infected Earthlings and helping Earth and Earthlings in the future, caused unprecedented enthusiasm and interest. We even found ourselves in difficulties — who to send to Earth — with so much demand."

Here the king could not resist and decided to interrupt the speaker. "Excuse me, please, for interrupting you. But let everyone fly who wishes to, if you have enough ships to send anyone who wants to. We Earthlings are very hospitable people and are always glad to have friends so let me hope that you can consider us as friends. There is enough space on the ground for everyone and the energy power source for your organism in our solar galaxy is very powerful. After all, we have the sun that will shine and heat Earth for at least another six billion years. The spectrum of solar radiation is very rich. So you can choose for yourselves the necessary wavelength for your nutrition and you are welcome to live with us for all six billion years!"

After a short pause, Smelan heard real human-approving laughter of the Committee members: "Oh, that would be just great! We have enough ships to evacuate all inhabitants of the star to other galaxies. As we mentioned, our star will soon end its existence, and we have already been exploring the galaxies for a long time in order to take our inhabitants away to a planet or star with suitable living conditions for us. Well, your offer is tempting for us... who knows, maybe Primleans would like to live with humans in a parallel world, to know all about you and to observe the development of your civilisation. It will be for us like a living reflection of our own history. After all, we were once at the same level of development as you are now, about five hundred thousand years ago.

"Well, we are beginning active preparations for our expedition to Earth and as soon as everything is ready, we'll let you know. We must complete the assembly of the satellite of Earth, which will create a protective bio-electromagnetic zone around the Earth, and it will take some time. In the meantime, we invite you to make more excursions to our star; you will be interested, we assure you."

"I am very grateful to you for everything and I would like to thank you, on behalf of all Earthlings, for your noble mission for the salvation of Earth and Earthlings, for your exploit." Smelan tried to shape his thoughts.

In the air, there emerged outlines of shimmering from gentle glowing of the rocks.

"Well, my thought has reached them, thought the king. "I shall look again at an extraordinary, magical star and then be ready to fly back home!" The king was just bursting with lots of different emotions: "Superbiotechs — their generosity, their so beautiful and mysterious star. They will be guests on Earth, and perhaps many of them will want to stay on Earth, and for them it will be their second home. They will exist in a parallel world with humans." Oh, from all this his head was just getting dizzy.

The king tried to calm himself but the excitement was still on the boil. Suddenly he heard the enchanting sounds of Earth: here rustled and whispered the leaves of the forest and the birds began to sing in it. Smelan even heard the babbling of the brook. The forest freshness and a subtle scent of woodland wild flowers suffused the air. He sniffed these odours with delight and recalled his favourite walks in the woods, fishing in the wild forest lakes, and he began to fall into a sweet drowsiness... He was not surprised at anything now. He knew that the biotechs were the real wizards, and he fell asleep under the cheerful twittering of birds.

Chapter 17

When the king woke up, he felt completely refreshed and rested. Now he was definitely ready to go on the tour. Only Smelan thought of this as his body gradually began to turn to a vertical position, and his space-suit slowly 'floated' to him. Then the suit itself helped the king to put it on. Finally, all the buckles and tubes were in place, the helmet 'floated' to him and hoisted itself onto his head. The milky cloud, in which he had stayed all this time, had gradually dissipated and the beautiful radiant star again appeared to King Smelan.

He heard a pleasant, a very Earthly voice, female this time: "Dear King Smelan, you have already seen our landscapes and have some idea of the north and south poles of Prima. However, you do not know how we live. You have also not seen our scientific and technical centres. Would you be interested to see it all?"

"Why, of course, of course," replied the king without hesitation. And they flew, or rather it was evident to the king that he was flying alone, but he constantly felt that he changed the direction of flight at someone's will. Again, rocks sparkling with emeralds and diamonds could be seen speeding away down below. "It is good that here there are no such pot-bellied and greedy monsters who infected our land today. Otherwise, they would quickly change the landscape of Prima," thought the king to himself. "Prima would be left like a desert after their invasion, no longer shining with anything."

They approached the rock, and after a moment he found himself in complete darkness. Gone was the shine and sparkle. In the helmet appeared a weak pleasant light. The voice said, "Here we are in the home of one of the Primleans. You will not see or hear anything, but believe me there is now the family together and even a lot of the neighbours looking at you. For the first time an Earthman is on the star Prima. You are our dear guest. Already every Primlean knows that you have arrived with a mission to save Earth, and many want to see, touch and talk with you. Would it be possible to answer at least a few questions?" the same voice asked.

"Of course, with great pleasure," Smelan formed his thought. Don't forget that the king was talking now mostly at the level of thoughts. He loved it; he found it helped him to focus and shape his thoughts in a brighter way. He even began to feel that his head began to work better and his brain tossed thoughts like pancakes as they flew out of his head — hot and round. His new skill was rather useful now as the family of Primleans and their friends didn't talk in human language.

Although the king saw or heard nothing, he felt different sensations and feelings come to him and flow through him. Sometimes he had a sudden desire to smile or even laugh, and sometimes he felt so amazingly pleasant and good as if he should sing or dance! He knew it was a biotech affecting him. "So that's what it will be like on Earth in a parallel world with biotechs," thought Smelan. "I wonder, I wonder…"

Suddenly he heard in his head the first question:

"Tell us, honoured King Smelan, how many people live on Earth?"

The king replied by sending a message, and added that there were that many people when he left but now, to the dismay of the Earthlings, people were turning into monsters pretty fast and he didn't know exactly how many people had kept human form. Then dozens of questions poured into his head… Primleans wanted to know about everything. They showed great interest in the nature of Earth, the climate, fauna and flora, wanted to know about technical progress and scientific achievements, and also asked who governed Earth. It was difficult to answer this last question because formulating such thoughts on this issue had proved very complicated for the king.

Some time passed and questions kept showering down like peas; Smelan replied in good faith and in some detail. After a while he felt very tired, and instantly the accompanying superbiotech invited him to finish the meeting and relax. The king's suit began to glow rosy-white which meant in the Primleans' energy language that the guest wanted to say goodbye and wish them all the very best.

Chapter 18

Then the suit began to take a horizontal position, and soon Smelan again saw gleaming diamond rocks and they gradually left the cave, home of one of the Superbiotech family. The voice in the suit told him that now all Primleans will be aware of his visit, and that this conversation with the family will be known to all and available for all Primleans wishing to learn a little about Earth.

It also said that the flight to Earth was planned for two days' time. In these days Smelan should rest and gather strength for the difficult and lengthy flight. But the superbiotech assured him that he need not worry at all as their interstellar ships carried equipment by means of which they could overcome all the unforeseen difficulties of the flight — magnetic storms, deadly radiation of pulsars, or unexpected dense swarms of meteorites in the galaxy. Besides the ships have a protective biological membrane capable of repulsing the attacks of the Antipodals.

Smelan silently in his mind thanked the Primlean and felt himself becoming drowsy. He relaxed, closed his eyes and immediately began to sink into a dream.

Chapter 19

Finally came the day of the flight. On this day, Smelan woke very early. There was a tray with a cup of fragrant coffee, his last breakfast on Prima. On the screen appeared a superbiotech who informed him that they were ready to begin preparations for launch. Also, he said that for the duration of the flight he would be transformed into a cloud, which would be enclosed in a protective suit. Antipodals would not be able to hit him, as had happened during the flight to the star Prima. A pleasant voice added that the flight would last for fourteen light-years.

The king was only a king, and not a scientist. He did not know how far one light-year is. He didn't know and didn't feel what changes he could expect to see in his native land and, it must be said, that light covers a distance of ten trillion kilometres during one light year, an inconceivable distance! Would you like to see how it looks in numbers? Are you ready? It's 10,000,000,000,000 km so you can see it's an impressive number isn't it? Just try to imagine how far away Earth was from them — fourteen x ten trillion kilometres! One's head is spinning from these trillions. For comparison you should know, my friend, that the distance from Earth to the Sun is a mere one hundred and fifty million kilometres — 150,000,000 km. Maybe, when you grow up, you'll be interested in all these millions and trillions and will be an astronomer or a captain of a spaceship! Then you'll remember this story.

However, the superbiotechs knew what Smelan could expect. They had made all the necessary cosmic calculations and concluded that the king would no longer have any remaining relatives — they would all have died long ago. After all, time flows differently, depending on what part of the universe you're in, what gravitational forces are acting on your star or planet, and the speed with which it moves in space. Therefore, being in different galaxies we grow and age differently. So for twins the age difference could be a hundred years, if we can imagine such an experiment and put them in different galaxies.

The Primleans did not want to upset the king before flying. Although emotions were unknown to them, they had analysed human nature and knew that people are susceptible to emotions. They see life as a series of feelings — coming and going. They may experience happiness, joy, they can laugh, but at the same time they may be very upset to experience setbacks and even to cry. Superbiotechs knew that, at this stage of humanoid development, senses are an inseparable part of life. This, of course, is the diversity of life and makes it like a colourful mosaic. However, superbiotechs acted properly at all times, and in the only way possible in terms of progress and the Absolute Good. The possibility of mistakes was excluded. Errors brought small and large losses, and would hinder the progress of development.

So, they decided it would be better to deliver the king safe and unharmed to Earth, and then, judging by what they would see there, help the king to accept life on Earth as it was. They could affect the brain and thoughts of a person and bring them to a state of calm and balance, if required. Primleans possessed all the secrets — these clever superbiotechs.

Chapter 20

Almost half of the entire population of Prima came to bid farewell to the ships flying to Earth. For the Primleans who were going to Earth there were very serious tasks: first to help Earthlings to destroy harmful Antipodals and set Earthlings free from them and also to protect them from future invasions and viruses. In addition, the Primleans were looking for a planet or star in different galaxies, which could be their homeland as their star was dying and in two hundred years would become a lifeless cosmic object with temperatures as low as Absolute Zero — which is -273 degrees Celsius. Can you imagine it? No, we cannot, we never experience such low temperatures on Earth. This is a property of space, where unthinkable things happen. Mind you, unthinkable for us ordinary people, but scientists have a great deal of knowledge about all this.

The Primleans were sure that they would succeed in finding a suitable planet or star in the universe as there are billions of galaxies and trillions of stars and planets. Then all the inhabitants of Prima would move there. Prima's twin star would have the same sad destiny. Sometimes they are called 'white-dwarf-twins' because these stars radiate dazzlingly bright light.

So, if the Primleans could find the energy conditions of Earth and Sun suitable for them, then with the invitation of the king they could find a homeland on Earth and live with Earthlings in a parallel world. This expedition was therefore extremely important not only for Earth and Earthlings but for the Primleans as well.

Chapter 21

The king, of course, did not see the Primleans, but, by seeing how quickly the rocks near the spaceport changed colour, he realised that he was among millions of Primleans who came to say farewell to the spaceships ready for the long journey. The king, though not a scientist, had noticed an interesting feature during the journey across Prima: when a group of superbiotechs was near the rocks they began to quickly change colour and shimmer like the stars in the sky. He thought it was rock crystals reflecting the Primleans' movement because Primleans were energetic figures and radiated considerable though invisible energy.

Smelan rolled his eyes, looking at all this beauty, and his heart ached from the flood of emotions. On the one hand he couldn't wait to get back home and meet with his family, to hug them, kiss, and tell of all his adventures. But on the other hand, he was sorry to leave this fabulous star with such kind, sympathetic and committed Primleans from whom so much could be learned. However, duty called the king — to save Earth from capture.

Inside the suit was heard a voice. It said that the king would now hear all the necessary information about the flight and could then ask questions. "So," continued the voice, "one thousand spaceships will be sent to Earth, and there will be one hundred Primleans in each ship. They must cover the distance of one hundred and forty trillion kilometres. It's the distance of fourteen light-years but, in terms of human calculations and understanding, it will be about twenty-seven years".

"Twenty-seven years!" thought the King, "Twenty-seven years! But this means I will probably be absent from my home for about fifty-four years because I have to multiply twenty-seven years by two! Good Lord! Then I should be a very old man now! And plus, the time I've spent on Prima... But it felt to me that I was absent for maybe a couple of months? I don't have a mirror but my hands — look at them — they are still young! And my legs — they are still strong! How strange this all is. How differently time flows in different parts of galaxies... Oh, my brain is confused again."

The king hadn't the slightest clue about all these numbers but decided not to ask about them now, since the space centre was, of course, very busy preparing everything for launch. Yes, these figures were for him an abstract concept, and he didn't know that the twenty-nine light-years' distance of the flight for him would take about seventy to ninety years on Earth. Of course, he wouldn't find any of his living relatives. It was a blow that would have been hard to bear, so the Primleans hadn't said anything about this to

Smelan. The king needed all his strength for the flight, a lot of strength!

The voice also confirmed that for the duration of the flight the king would be turned into a biological cloud and shut in a special container that would protect him on the journey. So, if the king had no questions, then they could begin the process of transformation at once. To tell the truth, Smelan had dozens of questions in his head, but he felt that from extreme excitement he couldn't concentrate and form clear and sharp thoughts to send to the Primleans. He decided to rely on such amazingly perfect Primleans and become a cloud. "Besides," thought Smelan, "I was once a cloud and I even liked it in some ways. It's good for a change sometimes, to feel so light, airy and carefree like a cloud. Let them transform me and... God help me in my wanderings." Transform. King Smelan sent his thought.

The king had noticed that his arms and legs were getting lighter and weightless and somehow disappearing, and soon he felt light and airy. "All done, I'm again His Majesty the Cloud King," smiled Smelan to himself.

The flight was proceeding according to plan. Superbiotechs had foreseen all possible complications and attacks by hostile beings. All the thousands of spaceships had strong electromagnetic protection that could change the trajectory of any attacking object and prevent a collision. Or, if forced by circumstances, then simply destroy the object and turn it into space dust... Also, they had radiation equipment which could neutralise any biological attacks, both viral and bacterial, or parasitic. Therefore, these chosen inhabitants of the universe were about to reach Earth safe and unharmed.

Chapter 22

On approaching Earth, the council in charge of the project gathered in the leading ship. Prior to the meeting, the captain had collected data on the situation on Earth; before starting the awakening of the king they had to make a decision — what and how to say to Smelan that there were no longer any people on Earth. Nobody! All of his friends, relatives and those close to him would all be long dead or turned into these disgusting crawling grey creatures.

The Primleans certainly knew that this news might just kill the king immediately; his heart would not withstand the grief. After all, people greatly reduced their lifetimes because of sad feelings and worries. But what to do: they didn't yet have a sufficiently developed brain to control senses and convert them into energy, which on the contrary would add years to life, and not shorten it.

The historian of Earth, who was present at the council, suggested that, as soon as possible, they should send a radiation probe to check the burials of the king's relatives and people close to him. If they had followed all the rules of burial, those honoured like royalty were placed in a pyramid, so this then was a great chance to revive them. For superbiotechs this wouldn't be a problem at all.

They would transfer the family of the king to another time-dimension and would return them to their years. This would be the salvation of King Smelan and of humanity.

The captain and the other members of the Committee supported this idea and expressed their hearty approval. Immediately researchers started on the implementation of this project. A few hours later, Beta probe was ready for launch. The answer came almost at once, and to their great satisfaction the answer was positive for biotechs. Yes, now they would be able to help the king and the future of humanity! Yes, now they could start the procedure for waking Smelan. Earth on the illuminated screen had looked the size of a blue orange. Soon they would need to prepare for orbiting the Earth.

Chapter 23

The king opened his eyes. He instantly regained consciousness, he might already be on Earth, and he could perhaps already be at home. Feelings overwhelmed him, the thought, flashed through his head faster than the wind. Gradually he began to feel his body and pretty soon saw that he was in his chair; the image in front of him was the green lawn of his garden. The king was so excited that he couldn't concentrate enough, to ask a single question.

He heard a voice he knew, and which had become familiar. "Relax, Your Majesty, we are already orbiting the Earth. Our long and difficult flight is over; we avoided attacks from Antipodals, but had to deviate from the original route because of a dense cluster of meteorites in a neighbouring galaxy to Earth. We went around the galaxy, and stayed for three Earth-years, and due to this action, all of our ships arrived intact.

"We must now adapt to the local climatic and biological conditions, and make the necessary technical preparations for this. Yes, yes, continued the voice quietly, "we know that you, Your Majesty, will be eager to leave the ship and see your family and your people. But do not rush especially; you will also need to adapt."

There was a pause. Suddenly the king felt a first slight prick in the heart, and then it was as if it collapsed into a black abyss. He sensed trouble. "Your Majesty," continued the same magically calm voice, "This is the moment when you have to call upon all your courage and spirit and gather together the wisdom of the ages to accept sad news."

Again, there was a pause, but now the king felt as if his body were being filled with iron. His misgivings and fears were as if suspended from him and hung in the distance like black spiny clusters. He was gaining the unbending spirit of the royal ancestors. He was ready to hear the truth.

The biotech told him his name. "You know me, in fact my voice, not me, Your Majesty. I accompanied you on the star Prima and now I shall be with you all the way ahead on Earth." Nuri — this was the biotech's name, good old Nuri — told him the history of Earth and his family for the last eighty years. It turned out that Smelan had been away for eighty years!

At first the king was shocked that so many years had flown by since his journey. It has been mentioned earlier that time flows differently on Earth and in space. For example, two or three years for a man in space could turn into hundred or so years for people on Earth.

Of course, man cannot live so long, and the entire royal family — a wife and a daughter and even grandchildren — were buried with honourable custom in the royal tomb. Besides, without the king's support they wouldn't have survived because of the invasion by the Antipodals. It was the first tragic news.

The second was even more shattering! On Earth, there remained no normal people. They had all been infected and turned into the terrible grey thick scaly monsters. They ate all the animals, and those they couldn't catch died out because the trees, grass and flowers and everything were trampled and eaten by scalies. Earth had become a bleak dusty desert with revolting hobbling and crawling monsters.

It was now impossible for the king to survive in this dusty, shattered, and once-flourishing, homeland. Smelan fell silent. From the shock, he could neither collect his thoughts, nor speak. The staunch royal spirit that he had felt recently began to leave him. He suffered deep trauma and Nuri noted that physical strength and a clear consciousness were leaving Smelan rapidly. Everything must be done to avoid this. The king was the sole hope for mankind. Nuri contacted the headquarters of the expedition, and it was decided to put the king to sleep and then do the necessary reviving and stimulating procedures.

So, very positive news was received. The entire royal family, despite the millions of grey scalies, had been buried with all royal honours and most importantly in the place which was out of reach by grey freaks — in pyramids. This gave the biotechs great hope for the revival of the royal family.

Chapter 24

The team wasted no time setting to work. First of all, they'd be occupied with Smelan. They told him the plan of action. First they'd restore the king's health and then proceed to the recovery of normal life on Earth — with forests full of animals, rivers full of all sorts of fish, fields on which to grow vegetables and cereals, orchards full of fruit trees and, most importantly, Earth would again be inhabited by people. and the king would see many of his family — his wife, his daughter and grandchildren. It wouldn't be possible to see them all but only those that were buried in the pyramids.

The king listened and could not believe his own ears; it was like a fantasy story. He gathered all the strength of his weakening body and sent the question: "How long will it take me to heal and how long is required to restore life on Earth?"

Nuri replied that the recovery of the king would not take long. First, he would be put to sleep and, with the help of curative radiation, rebuild his cells, the brain cells and the organs. Two days later, he would wake up and would continue the recovery process with the expedition doctor. By the end of the week he should be as healthy and full of strength and energy as he maybe ever was.

"Though the healing of the planet and return of life on Earth will take very much longer, about a year, and maybe more. This is the expected timeframe. All we need now is your consent to our plan. If you think that our plan will lead to good progress, then send us your thoughts. But if you think it is too difficult and an impossible task for you, then also send us your thoughts. Think about it, King Smelan, and take your time to answer. I repeat again, at times it will be very difficult and dangerous for you."

The king became thoughtful. For him it was a familiar occupation. When he ruled the kingdom, he had to think a great deal in order to see the problems and make wise decisions. Now he was expected to make an exceptionally important decision: to restore the normal blossoming life on Earth or to be idle and die of grief and abandon Earth to those vile, grey, greedy creatures.

"There is no hesitation in my heart," thought the king. "Whatever efforts are required of me, however difficult and dangerous it is, I have to participate in the revival of life on Earth and to be with the superbiotechs. This is my royal duty; it is my duty to mankind." He sent his thought to Nuri and the whole Committee. In response, the screen appeared before him with a thousand cheerful, shimmering specks of light. The Superbiotechs rejoiced with Smelan over his decision.

"So we come to the realisation of our project," the king heard the voice of Nuri say. He replied, "I thank all Primleans, and you who have flown here, with heartfelt and great gratitude on behalf of the whole future of humanity!

"Well, and thanks be to God," — thought King Smelan out of habit.

PART TWO

Chapter 1

King Smelan opened his eyes, stretched his limbs and found himself feeling fine, just perfect, in fact he hadn't felt such an influx of energy, since, well, in his youth. He wanted to manage, reign, create, discuss scientific discoveries and dizzying construction projects, resolve difficult disputes between the continents, oh-oh, and many, many other urgent matters with which His Majesty was usually busy every day. He certainly did not forget anything. He knew that ahead of him awaited a very difficult time — weeks, months, and maybe years of intense struggle with these malign Antipodals.

However, he fully trusted the superbiotechs, who assured him that they knew how to clear the memory of the poor and creepy creatures and decode a bewitched brain. Our brain consists of millions of tiny cells which contain all the information about everything, and we call it memory. So the superbiotechs told the king that they could change the contents of these cells so as to destroy bad information or memory, and leave or even add, good information.

Depending on what information there is more of in our head — good or bad — we feel either very cheerful and jolly and happy, or weak and dull. So our head is good not only for hairstyles and hats but is like a queen of our 'kingdom' — the whole body. Treat her with respect and care, my friends.

The thoughts of the king were interrupted by Nuri. He appeared in the form of a hologram. You already know, my friends, what a hologram is — an image that accurately reproduces an object or person that is formed in the air with the help of lasers. It seems to float in the air — most curious.

Nuri informed the king that a great deal of information had already been received in all areas of the state of the Earth and Earthlings. He asked Smelan how he felt and whether he was ready to listen to all this news. The king replied that he was feeling fine and added that he had not felt so strong for a long time, well, as if he were twenty-five years old.

"We have restored you, Your Majesty, if I may say so, and now you are in the best possible form in which a person on Earth can be. Well, in that case, we will start work, and I will tell you everything you need to know at this stage. Also, with your consent, we will discuss further plans."

Chapter 2

"We have new ideas after the last survey of the land, and I'll tell you about them now. Firstly, we cannot animate and restore everything, absolutely everything and everyone — I mean the plant world and especially the people who died many years ago. Our tasks must be real. We will be able to help all the surviving ugly creatures restore their human appearance to everyone who has been turned by Antipodals into paunchy giants with pencil heads or miserable creeping scaly ones. They will again become beautiful people and will look wonderful and pleasing to Your Majesty.

"We have all the necessary biochemical technology and equipment for this so this is very important and good news. However, if we first restore these bewitched and miserable ones to the human form, they will appear on a completely deserted Earth, uninhabitable by people. You saw the pictures of the Earth and what it has turned into, a bare desert with creeping scalies... br-rrrr."

Here the king apologized and interrupted Nuri. He said that he had not seen the latest images of Earth and didn't know how it looked now!

"Is that so!" exclaimed Nuri. "You haven't been shown the latest pictures of the Earth and you do not know how all the seven continents look now?

"Yes, dear King Smelan, I'm sorry to tell you this, but continents have turned into dusty grey deserts from being green, full of life, full of beautiful animals, and butterflies, and flowers. There are strong winds blowing, forming sandstorms, and people could not survive in such a land. Only these half-dried scaly ones still scratch through the scanty deserts, and their fat bosses hide in the dug-out tunnels.

"Ah, well, we're not alienated to anything human," Nuri joked. "Forgetfulness, but this is fortunately not an attack of Antipodals on us. It's just that we have a lot of things to do now. All the people of Prima are extremely busy and there was an unfortunate mistake. I apologise, Your Majesty. I will immediately submit pictures to you. You will see them now, right here, on the hologram. But prepare yourself, be courageous and know that we will help your trouble; that is why we have come here."

Chapter 3

The Nuri hologram melted into the air. He gave the king time to think and prepare himself for seeing pictures of the Earth. A cup of sweet-smelling aromatic coffee came over to him on a tray. Smelan was very happy about this.

He sipped his coffee and tried to master the excitement. He mentally commanded all the cells of his brain to be cleared of fear and unrest. After all, it was just accumulation of bad energy and we, people, can by force of will destroy this negative energy and replace it with a bright, good positive one. So the king mentally poured good energy into his cells, and soon he felt strong and confident, ready to cope with everything he would now see.

As soon as he got stronger, he heard Nuri's voice. He asked him to start the show. "Start, Nuri, and thank you for your help." Smelan sent his thought. The king fidgeted in his very comfortable chair and prepared himself for terrible surprises.

What he saw, he already knew from the descriptions of Nuri, but nevertheless emotionally — the king after all remained a man — he was terribly depressed. It's one thing to know something in your head but quite another to see everything with your own eyes. Smelan could not restrain himself... he cried. He was strong and confident, but still the tears rolled down his cheeks. A few seconds later, he suddenly remembered the wisdom: 'Only the heart is sharp. What you see with your eyes is not the most important thing…'

"Yes, of course," the king told himself. I believe with all my heart that everything will be fine. I see it with my heart! Also, I feel that the cells of my brain are sending me the same thought." And King Smelan smiled, smiled broadly and with great hope in his keen heart.

Nuri emerged. "Your Majesty, you have coped perfectly with a difficult emotional task, you are the real King! Well, now it's time to decide what practical steps need to be taken to restore Earthlings on land. I said before that if we return human form to all the 'scaly ones', they will end up on deserted uninhabited land where there will be nothing to eat and it will be impossible to find food. There are only sand and dust storms.

"However, if we return all the wealth of its flora and animals and insects to the land first, then all these bewitched freaks will quickly reap all the plants and eat all the animals and birds because they now have a brutal appetite. There was nothing left on Earth for a long time and they ate everything. With the appearance of fresh greens and vegetables and fruit, they will breed with the speed of greenflies and bring to nothing all our efforts. Therefore, we came to an interesting idea and, if you agree with us, we will immediately begin to act.

"We paralyse all the scalies, all the fat creatures hiding in the underground passages, in short all the bewitched people turned into freaks. We have such biochemical means. We spray them on all continents and the biochemical gases will penetrate everywhere, even in the most seemingly inaccessible places — in all caves and underground passages, in all the cracks in the rocks. They will remain paralysed for as long as we need. They will stiffen in those poses in which they are overtaken by our biochemical gas. Do not worry, Your Majesty, this gas will not do them any harm, they will just be locked up for a while and will not move and look for food for themselves.

"In the meantime, we will restore the green cover of the Earth, its wonderful animals, and birds, and everything, everything you know, but not revive people yet.

"As I have already mentioned, it will be impossible to restore all vegetation and all the varieties of birds and animals. Nature, your Earthly nature, has incredible power. With our push, our help, it will start to supplement and reproduce the missing plants and animals. Nature is very clever and very patient, but you people must all help her as soon as you can, so that everyone will live happily here in your beautiful big house that you call the Earth."

Nuri was talking for a long time about all these ideas and he saw that Smelan needed to rest at least a little; he said goodbye to him and promised to drop by as soon as he saw from the sensors that the king felt bright again.

After a short rest, Nuri saw that the king could continue the conversation, and he appeared in the air. Smelan nodded his head and smiled. He said that he was ready to talk, but he had one very important request and he would like to know the opinion of the superbiotechs. Nuri immediately guessed: "Dear Smelan, we know that you can't wait to find out about your family and friends; please calm down and don't worry. They will be all right. However, everything must happen in order.

"First, we restore the vegetation on Earth, then return the human form to all the bewitched creatures and only then can we come close to do the job on your family and friends. This way will be better because, when they become alive again, they will see, not a desert and bewitched freaks, but normal people and green Earth. Don't you think so?

"As we have already told you, we will not have problems with them; since they are in the pyramids, their genetics have not undergone terrible changes and we will just start the time machine and return them to be healthy and well. Do not worry, Your Majesty, and rely on us — everything will be not only good, but excellent!"

"Ah, I still cannot find such expressive and bright words to thank you. You are an amazing civilisation, and the world will never lose hope of gaining the path of goodness and light when you are in the universe."

"Maybe, maybe," Nuri replied. "We also like Earthlings very much; you have good hearts and good intentions. We will be happy to coexist with you in a parallel world, if you want it."

Chapter 4

"So, Your Majesty, we are proceeding to the first stage of the salvation of the Earth. After spraying the gas on the first continent, which will paralyse all bewitched creatures, we will begin to restore the animals and birds and plants. Soon this continent will turn green. This will be our first step in the struggle and confrontation with the Antipodals.

"You know, they have already decided that they completely subordinated the land to themselves. They sucked a colossal amount of light kind energy from people and provided themselves with food for thousands of years. They will store this energy in special energy systems. The Earth turned into a lifeless desert and they no longer needed it. Now they have only to prepare for their return flight. Antipodals do not yet know that we've arrived, since we have made ourselves invisible as an energy object.

"What would you like to do, Your Majesty, while we restore the green world?"

"Nuri, without a doubt I'd like to help you as much as I can!"

"We'll think about it, and thank you for your offer. I shall talk to the Committee and come back to you soon.

In a while, Nuri returned and said, "We considered your offer of help and found it would be useful if you were to take an orbital flight after the green blanket and animal world of each continent (one by one) have been restored.

"What I want to say, Your Majesty, is that, of course, we have all the maps of the Earth, we have historical information, and we know how she looked at different periods of her life; it's clear how beautiful and fertile the planet was," continued Nuri. "However, your eyes can see obvious inaccuracies... Well, for example, maybe a lion will stand next to an antelope and smile at her, or a hare will play with foxes, and a cat with a mouse and... and so on... that for us would be natural in everyday life because there are no enemies at all. For your era, such companionship may be unacceptable and incompatible... for the time being.

"Besides, you, Your Majesty, could do a great service to the whole revived humanity and think about how to arrange a festival on Earth after its return to life, after its expanses are again covered with green meadows, and the forests full of different animals and birds. In cities on the streets there will be beautiful people again, and there will not be a single scraping scaly freak. Only you can think of such a holiday, because only people know how to arrange such a holiday over the whole Earth. It will be a grandiose event and the celebration also needs to be grandiose, because this day/week/year will go down in history as the second birth of the Earth, as the resurrection of the Earth itself and its inhabitants.

"It will not be easy to plan such a celebration; there will be so much to think about, to prepare and execute. You, of course, know best how to entertain people in the best possible way, how to surprise them and amaze them. Maybe the most fantastic thing will be the very fact of people's return to life, and their meeting with friends and relatives.

"You can also introduce us, and tell about us everything you want, and also ask the whole population of the Earth whether they agree to live with us in a parallel world. You ask me how you will introduce us for we are invisible! However, for a short time we can make ourselves visible, especially if you choose a place where we will have rocks rich in minerals behind us. When we move, or think, or communicate, we radiate energy. This radiation, reflected from the minerals, will cause glowing and flickering."

"It will be so beautiful! I had already seen this multi-coloured glow when I was on the star Prima."

"Well, here, yes, it will be like that, only a little weaker. After all, rocks on Prima are thousands of times richer than on Earth because of the processes of crystallisation. Our rocks, you could say, are gold and silver with deposit of diamonds, rubies, and sapphires. However, we do not make jewellery from all this, we use them in super technologies to make progress and improve the life of the Primleans, make it interesting and useful."

Nuri also said that the king can assure people that the superbiotechs will not interfere in the life of Earthlings in any way, only if the events are on the verge of disaster. Then the Council of Primleans and people will assemble. The situation will be discussed, and measures for rescue, or neutralisation, or diplomacy will be found.

Chapter 5

The king was delighted with the idea that he could help and was especially encouraged by the idea of a festival for the rebirth of mankind. He wondered how it had never occurred to him. Maybe subconsciously he was not as sure of success as the Primleans; he did not know practically all their possibilities, did he? King Smelan was not a scientist, and everything that he was told by the Primleans he just believed.

He recalled, it seemed it was quite recently, how he and the government approved the celebration of the day of HUMANITY, which was the cessation of all wars over the whole Earth.

It took the King a lifetime to achieve it but he devoted himself to this most important idea. Success was difficult, at times it seemed impossible; wars broke out in one corner of the Earth, then in another. Some countries had been at war not only for years, but for decades. Millions of young people died or returned from the war crippled and became disabled for life. The king was very grieved! It was necessary to stop wars and conflicts at all costs. For this it was worth trying and worth living.

So King Smelan set to work. Much effort and negotiation were made. The King visited every, even the smallest, country on Earth. He spoke with each people and urged them to learn to live without weapons, without violence, as befits intelligent beings to live.

Many years passed before all wars and conflicts died down. The borders between the states were gradually erased and, finally, disappeared altogether.

On the Earth one nation was formed, a human nation.

Over the whole Earth the day of the celebration of Humanity was declared.

And just as the Earthlings began to feel themselves in a new way, they felt happy and joyful and just when there were no more wars and strife, a new trouble struck, the biological attack of the Antipodals.

Chapter 6

Nuri knew from the report of the historian of the Earth what kind of difficulties Earthlings had endured, and what incredible efforts all governments and all the people had made to achieve the agreement on the cessation of all wars and conflicts over the whole Earth. He decided to talk to the Committee for saving the Earth about how to reward King Smelan and Earthlings. They deserved the glory of the universe because life on a planet without wars is worth remembering in future generations.

"Here again," thought the king. "It was necessary to gather my thoughts, martial my strength and, together with the superbiotechs to save the Earth and the people, and in the end to arrange a great celebration on Earth.

He began to think: now he was alone, no government, no family, and no support of the population. "Everything has to be done by myself." However, he did not despair. Yes, the task was difficult, but the spirit was excited, and it was necessary to arrange a feast not only with the mind but with the heart...

Yes, Smelan had to think about how to arrange a festival over the whole Earth, from north to south and from east to west. The people of the kingdom were very fond of all sorts of sporting events —

horse racing, for example, and in the north, sleigh riding with reindeer, and in the south, even more fun — to swim long distances across the ocean on the backs of dolphins, that have long become human fellows, and they've even learned to communicate with each other. The language of communication consisted of a set of sounds, body movements and sending simple thoughts. So the foundations of the dolphin language arose, and children began to study it at school. Every year the language grew richer, and people hoped that in the near future they would have parties with dolphins in the ocean.

In addition, the old ball game — football — was still very popular on all continents. Indeed, there are many more sports which both children and adults are very fond of...

What sport do you like my friends?

Well, our king was still going over the various amusements in his mind that his people were fond of. "It would be nice to arrange masquerade balls and festivities on all continents in the evening as well."

In the north, people would have put on terrible masks with horns and fangs and animal skins over their clothes. In ancient times such masquerade figures mercilessly rattled huge bells and whipped with whistling leather lashes to frighten and disperse evil spirits, y-yoh, what a terrible spectacle...

In the south, in Europe, it would be good to arrange fancy dress balls where women would flaunt lush silk dresses and masks of smiling beauties, and men would wear the suits of rich men and princes of different centuries.

In the east, people always want to hold festivities in the company of dragons made of bright silk and coloured paper with a mouth breathing fire that also drove away evil spirits. In the air they would launch thousands of coloured flashlights. "Fly, fireflies, we send hello and good wishes to the whole world."

You may know that people of different nations in ancient times held rituals for the expulsion of evil spirits. Everyone was afraid of them, because they brought misfortune to a person or family, and people always tried to get rid of them, not to admit them to a family home or to their souls...

In Africa, for example, people would certainly have lit fires and painted their bodies frighten evil spirits, and begun to dance military wild dances around the fire, to frighten and disperse all evil and impure forces.

"Yes," contemplated Smelan. "Many great games, and contests, and rituals have been preserved from ancient time. It's good, we should not forget our history — where we came from and what we went through. I probably need to just send the message to different corners of the globe after people regain their face and figure. I will tell them that we will celebrate the rebirth of mankind, and I will say on what day. This day can last a whole week or a bit longer... Week of happiness and joy! And let the local government decide for themselves

what masquerades and festivities to arrange —
they will have a big choice. Yes, it will be very
important to give a name to this holiday, hmm-
hmm... maybe 'HAPPY SMILING HOLIDAY', or
'EARTH REVIVAL' or... one needs to think, think
carefully and also arrange a competition on all
continents for the best name."

What would be your suggestion, friends?

Chapter 7

So many hours have passed in joyful reflections about the coming festivities, and the king was a little tired. After all, when you think very hard, you too get tired, although your body doesn't make any movements. Then we need a rest. You can walk in the park and listen to the singing of birds, play football, or go by bike to your friends, or you can go for a walk with the dog on the beach or play basketball on the court. Then your body will magically return you a lot of energy, and you can again load your brain with work.

The king so far had very limited space — no park nearby, no seas with seagulls, and of course no football or cricket. What to do? He was helped earlier by the bio-technicians, but they were now extremely busy, the king thought, and it was not a good idea to disturb them.

Meanwhile the Primleans split up into groups. So one group had now started the first stage and was spraying gas all over the Earth to paralyse the scaly ones. Another group was still assembling a temporary orbital house-ship from the spaceships that had flown to Earth from Prima. Everyone was very busy.

Then Smelan remembered the ancient yoga. These exercises already existed for thousands of years, and in the kingdom, children were taught at school this amazing and very effective system of regaining one's energy. You do not need to go anywhere. However, in order to succeed, you need patience and the ability to concentrate. If you think that you have patience, then you can receive, as if by magic, a lot of energy.

So Smelan began doing yoga exercises to shake off fatigue and gain energy. After half an hour of various exercises, he felt rested and cheerful. The king returned to his task of what to do first.

Chapter 8

The next day, Nuri appeared himself and asked Smelan about his thoughts and plans. The king told him what he had come up with.

Nuri said that from his point of view the plan was not bad, but there were some unreachable tasks at the moment. He laid them out. According to him, making masks, getting skins and sewing millions and millions of silk dresses would be problematic, since it would take a lot of different synthetic materials that could be produced only in factories that still needed to be built, and the biotechnicians simply didn't have time for this now. First and foremost, one needed to restore the appearance of people who had been turned into ugly creepy creatures and fat beasts with pumpkin bellies.

Instead, perhaps it would be better and certainly less wasteful to organise sports and activities. This was a good idea indeed. In the evenings there would be campfires on the streets and squares; people would dance, sing, listen to the music, and everywhere there would be beautiful illuminations and hologram performances. "We would help you with the illuminations — we are great masters at this — and you will see an extraordinary performance. We have all the necessary equipment and great experience to arrange an unforgettable holographic performance over the whole Earth. Let it be a surprise for you."

King Smelan agreed with pleasure.

"Now, Your Majesty, get ready for a sightseeing tour. Yesterday we sprayed gas and paralysed the scalies and their superiors — the fat creepy ones. So today, for now, you will see a sad, sad picture but these pictures will go into the history of Earth. I hope you do not fall into despair."

Smelan was ready for the excursion. He knew what to expect. However, with the assurance of Nuri, he felt much stronger now.

So they went for a low flight; Smelan saw crowds of paralysed, as if frozen, different sizes and shapes of 'scaly' and ungainly pot-bellied creatures with long narrow heads resembling sharpened pencils. They peeked out of all the cracks and tunnels and gathered in groups. The picture was frightening; the king never even imagined before what an incredible number of these unfortunate freaks were scattered across the land.

He was sad, of course, but now, with a belief in the future, he coped much better looking at this horrifying picture. He took many photographs, so that future generations would know about this catastrophe on Earth.

Only in the evening did they return 'home', to a huge flying station, which the Primleans had almost finished assembling from several spaceships that had flown from Prima. This huge 'house' was now in orbital flight around Earth and served Primleans both as a dwelling and as a scientific and technical centre.

Now near the Earth the king started to be hungry, but he felt uncomfortable admitting this to Nuri. Of course, the Primlean knew everything himself; he, as you already know, did not need words. He offered Smelan supper, a 'tube' dinner and, of course, his favourite cup of coffee. Smelan liked the dinner very much; it seemed to him unusually tasty. He had artichokes for a snack, then a carrot and coriander soup, and his favourite apple pie for dessert. All this was in tubes, but the king recognised the taste of these dishes, in spite of the paste from the tubes.

Nuri visited Smelan again after he had eaten and rested. He wished him good night and promised to drop by the next morning. Smelan fell into a sound healthy sleep and for the first time with a smile on his wise and tired face. He probably saw in a dream that the project was becoming a reality, and that everything, everything would be fine! "I thank you, kindest Primleans," said Smelan to himself.

Chapter 9

However, the Primleans did not sleep. That same night they began blocking the Antipodals' spaceship. They took them captive in a strong magnetic field and cut off communication with Earth. In addition, with the help of different radiations, they blocked all equipment inside the ship itself. So the Antipodal ship became completely their captive. They now had to decide what to do with it. Urgently, early at dawn the Council of the Primleans gathered. A whole star system in a faraway galaxy with a dark, negative past was their concern now. This galaxy was the principal enemy of the world, and enemy of kindness and joy. Unhappy, they didn't know the concept of love and friendship in life. What they did to the Earth proved their evil nature.

So the Council decided to stop the activity of the Antipodals on their station. They knew how to do this — they would stop the time inside the station. When time does not flow, everything seems to freeze; nothing changes and no one changes, and this means a complete standstill — as if there is a ship but there isn't because it is completely outside time.

The next step was to find a 'wormhole' — a path through the universe — and when they had time, to launch the Antipodal ship through this hole into another galaxy and another time dimension. There, who knows, they might be turned into other good creatures of the universe under different conditions and different time dimensions. It would be indeed a lucky end to the whole Antipodal story.

This was the plan and they wanted to tell the king first about all of this and ask his opinion.

Chapter 10

While physicists and astrophysicists were looking for ways to isolate the Antipodal ship, another group of Primleans, biologists, went on expeditions across the Earth to collect surface samples — dust, stones — anything that could be useful for identifying and restoring the genetics of humans, as well as animals and plants.

The Primleans hoped to find in the collected earth rocks the molecules of the genetic chains of all the disappeared animals and plants. Their task was to collect as much data as possible about the entire disappeared world. Within a few days they had assembled a huge store of data, and they started laboratory research.

In addition, a third group was also created, which was to collect data on the energy of the Earth and the sun, to determine the possibility of life for the Primleans on Earth in a parallel world with people. It was this group that made an unexpected discovery, which set the plan for the coexistence of the Primleans on Earth in great doubt.

Chapter 11

The problem was that the Primleans appeared to be visible in the sun! Strangely enough Smelan was the first to notice them when flying around the Earth. He saw how the little multi-coloured lights fluttered like butterflies, as if hopping on the surface of the Earth. Wherever he looked, he saw everywhere these little fireflies of different shapes. He thought maybe they were the fireflies of God? But he'd never noticed anything like this before. He thought that maybe after visiting God and Prima, he'd developed special abilities which he didn't have before? All this was very surprising and incomprehensible. King Smelan decided to ask the superbiotech what he thought — because the superbiotechs knew literally EVERYTHING!

Iyer — the king's new friend — was busy with the equipment; of course Smelan didn't see him, but he knew that as soon as he thought about contact with the superbiotech, he would immediately get in touch. Almost immediately, Iyer appeared as a hologram and Smelan asked him a question. He replied that he would immediately contact a group of biologists and an energy group who were exploring opportunities for life on Earth.

Smelan saw that the picture on the hologram began to flash and quickly change in colour. "Yes," thought he, "it turns out I noticed something important and now I find out what it is." Soon the hologram 'calmed down' and in a voice similar to that of the king himself, Iyer calmly confirmed this fact that the Primleans become visible to man in sunlight.

He also said that they would notify the Committee for the Salvation of Earth (CSE) and would discuss this news with the king. But, said Iyer, this would not affect the program to restore life on Earth. This fact only concerned a possible prospect for the Primleans to stay on the Earth or not. Both Primleans and the king himself should think about this. As soon as both sides were ready to discuss this issue, they would take care of this, but now there were more urgent things to do.

Chapter 12

Smelan was shocked, of course. He did not expect something like this, but said to himself "Don't worry, calm down." When he'd calmed down, only then could he begin to analyse the situation. In the meantime, he couldn't refrain from asking Iyer questions.

"Dear Iyer, I know you are very busy, but before I start to think about it, I would like to ask just one question."

"No problem, Your Majesty."

"I saw these jumping and flying fireflies; they all had different configurations — I saw mostly spherical shapes but also some were in the form of boats with long lateral legs or tentacles, some reminded me of trees, and some looked like flowers that bowed in all directions as if in the wind. Yes, I have seen many more such different silhouettes; it's hard for me even to describe everything. What are these? Are they all Primleans?"

"Yes, dear King. They are. Primleans have the ability to change their silhouettes. It is impossible even to determine all forms and quantities. They change them every day, and every hour and minute. This is their life game. Above all, it is also the language of communication. It would be complicated for you to follow it but for Primleans it's necessity plus fun. The Primleans read each other by a changing of colour or configuration. You will never see a still form or colour — everything constantly changes. You change a fashion in clothes in your lives, and we change ourselves, more practical, and you don't need to spend money buying clothes or making them, or build factories producing them. We're very economical and sophisticated," added Iyer.

For the king, this was another new thing, difficult to understand — a beautiful live superbiotechs' game of constantly changing self-radiation. It's like our words — we change them to express our thoughts. While they don't write or print anything, they create and show everything of themselves while on the move.

Nope, the king clearly didn't want to part with such enchanting guests. One must find a way out. What could it be? If they lived in cities it would be a great shock to folk; people were not as yet ready for such communication.

"Ah, my cloudy head. I think I've found the way out. We've a lot of deserts on Earth. It's too hot there and there are no trees, no grass, no flowers, no gardens — it's exactly what the people of Prima are used to! There nobody will see them; no one will go to live in a desert even for a million tugri. People don't like deserts and cannot survive there even for two days — they would burn in the sun or die from thirst without water. I will propose this idea to the

Star Committee! "Hurray," exclaimed the king, "an excellent idea! Aha, my cloudy head, sometimes you are as clear as a blue sky. Thank you, my good old grey one."

Chapter 13

Smelan had a lot on his hands; preparing for the celebration had to be thought of. All this required order in the head. First the king decided to make a plan for the routine of each day. Only in this way was it possible to achieve success. He began to work hard.

The day would start with morning exercises, then a light breakfast, followed by work on organising the celebration. A tube-type lunch in the afternoon would go down well. It was necessary for the king to meditate after lunch to make his head work well, ingeniously. Besides, he had to train his head to transmit thoughts to Primleans. Thoughts should be brief and clear, and then the Primleans would understand them without mistakes. It's easy to say everything that comes to mind, but it's not a royal style. The king must be at the royal level — meaning the highest — brief, clear, and convincing.

In the meantime, all urgent steps were being made by the Primleans. It was time to gather all the groups together with King Smelan, tell him about everything and discuss the next stage and the next steps. Smelan also prepared for the meeting with the Primleans — he had something to say and offer them.

The Primleans checked on the king's abilities — whether he might be too tired; fed him with high calorie tube-type food which, by the way, he liked very much, and arranged a meeting for one Earthly day. The meeting was to take place in the main compartment of the orbiting 'house', and was scheduled for Monday. The Primleans learned that all the major events on Earth began on a Monday. So, it was to be on 04.04.3099 on the Earth calendar.

The Monday came, the fourth of April, 3099. In the morning Smelan woke up as usual at six o'clock. A minute later his cup of coffee appeared. Interestingly, it was the same cup that first 'swam up' to him on the prima star. It turned out that it travelled with him through all the galaxies and survived, and had become already his usual 'good old' morning cup. It was nice, very nice to drink from it fragrant coffee, as if he was meeting an old friend...

Someone should be on the way to collect him for the committee meeting. Smelan did not now need a spacesuit. The superbiotechs had created terrestrial conditions for the king inside the ship — the temperature was pleasant, about twenty-two degrees, normal air pressure, no rain, and very clean air with a small admixture of ozone, like air on Earth after a thunderstorm, light and smelling delicious. Such air filled your lungs with joy, and your head with clear thoughts.

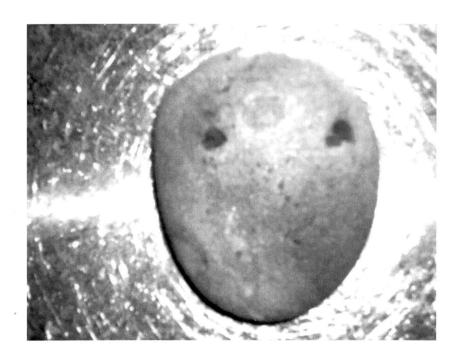

Just as Smelan thought that he was pretty well ready for the meeting, the hologram appeared. But now there was not a meadow and its Royal Oak on the hologram but something that looked like a stone face. The 'face' started to talk in Nuri's voice. Yes, it was Nuri! So it turned out that if he could look like this and all Primleans could look like this too, then a person could see them with the naked eye. It was interesting, oh how interesting. "How do they do it?" the king thought excitedly.

Of course, Nuri had read the king's thoughts and said: "Your Majesty, you know we can do wonders from your point of view, but these are just the laws of physics. We simply switched to a different wavelength using the adaptor we installed on the ship. We don't need to be visible to ourselves, as you know, but today will be a very important meeting. You are not familiar with the rest of the committee's superbiotechs, and therefore, for the sake of familiarity and your convenience, we will all be visible today... kind of. However, we decided that for communication it is enough to show only our 'portraits', if I may say so, very similar to those you had in your palace, for example. The rest of our 'looks' will only distract you from discussion and decision-making. For you it will be easier to communicate just with portraits."

The king remembered what intricate figures he had seen during the flight around the Earth, and in his mind, he agreed with Nuri. He said out loud: "Of course, Nuri, I understand and am in total agreement with you. Today we must make important decisions. Well, let us 'sail', my dear Nuri, and thank you very much for everything you do for me."

"It's a great honour for me," Nuri said. We all do it for you and the Earth, because we cannot behave differently, Smelan. This is the meaning of our existence.

Mmm... something more..." he hesitated, "I would like to say a few words about our portraits: I think from your terrestrial point of view, we all have 'faces' of 'stone'." But we are from the stone planet, are we not? We do not have any green grass, no beautiful flowers, no mighty trees... we have only stones, pebbles, gems, diamonds...

that's probably why our heads sometimes look mmm... mmm stony, dare one say." Nuri kept a pause. "Well, let's 'fly', Your Majesty."

Chapter 14

The door of the king's cabin began to slide smoothly inside the wall, and the king went to the important and unknown meeting. He felt that he was being directed by Nuri, and the king turned right or left, and sometimes even jumped up slightly. Smelan did not walk and did not fly, but soared and advanced smoothly forward. You know, don't you, that all objects including people are weightless in the orbital station and everything seems to hang in the air. This seems very funny. If, for example, you let go of your cup of coffee, then it will not fall down and smash, it will not go anywhere, but will hang in front of you as if saying 'drink me, drink me.' What a miracle!

I strongly advise you, when you grow up, go into space and fly around the Earth for a few days to experience all these wonders for yourself. There are masses of them! However, you have to be fit to go into space, so start your training soon, my friends.

Or maybe you, dear reader, could start writing about space too. Imagine, just remember that everything, and you yourself, will be hanging in the air and won't fall anywhere but do somersaults all around you — the tricks of space.

So, Smelan now faced such wonders every day. At first everything was very unusual for him, and sometimes even inconvenient. For example, at first he couldn't sleep in his bed fastened to it — one can't turn or curl up —but if you do not buckle up, you'll just fly away to some compartment like a piece of fluff and get lost in the huge orbiting ship. The king learned to sleep fastened up; he had already learned a lot and became almost a trained cosmonaut. However, he continued to observe the wonders of weightlessness, continued to be surprised and to learn how to live in new conditions.

Smelan and Nuri approached the hatch of the cabin, where the Committee gathered. Nuri asked the king whether he was ready. He nodded. Nuri opened the hatch, and they 'sailed' into the spacious cabin.

In the first instant King Smelan saw nothing and no-one except the numerous flickering lights of the equipment that were mounted in the walls. However, soon the silhouettes of the portraits of participants appeared in a soft light. There were seven of them.   They really resembled a 'stone' style as Nuri had said.

The king introduced himself. He'd already, of course, appeared once, when he was on the star, Prima, but he did not know if they were the same Primleans now in front of him or completely different ones. The stone heads swayed and nodded.

"Our greetings to you, King Smelan," ran the message he received in his head. "Yes, we know you. You are the King of the kingdom of humanoids on the planet Earth of the solar system. We saw you and talked with you on our Prima star. And now we visit you as guests at your home. As Nuri said, we thought that today, in discussion, it would be more convenient and familiar for you to see at least our portraits rather than talk with 'emptiness' in your understanding."

"So first we will introduce ourselves." He suddenly heard a voice. Even the king shuddered from the unexpected sound. "Yes, Your Majesty, we have learned your language, and now we can communicate in the way you people do. We know you have made a lot of effort to communicate at the mental level; you started to do it very well indeed and you even got to like it. However, we don't mind speaking your language if you prefer and now you can relax." The king had just several seconds to bring himself round before the Committee started to introduce themselves:

1 The largest 'stone'-like head, as if with bulging eyes, swung, and the king heard a low voice: "I am the captain of the ship, Ay, Your Majesty."

2 The grey head with little holes looking like grey eyes as if on its forehead, and with a brown kind of mouth, swayed, and a kind voice said: "I am Ku, the head of the Committee for saving Earth and its people."

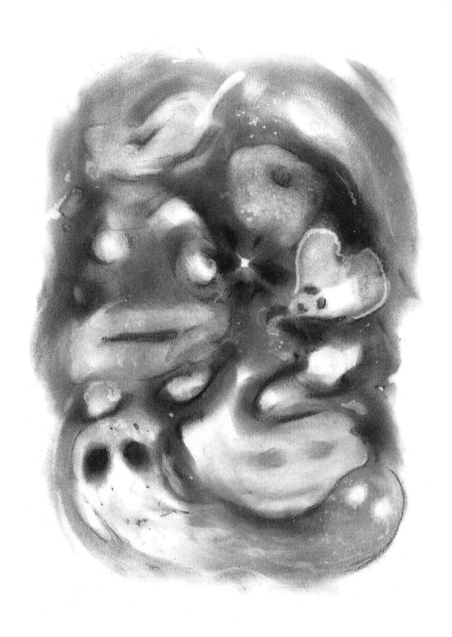

3 The next was a brown stone in the form of a smile with a dimple in the middle, and a tender, womanlike voice said, "I'm Issa and responsible for the planting of greens on the Earth."

4 Next, a 'stone' in the form of a human heart, swayed and as it were, a woman's melodic voice said: "I am Lol and I am responsible for restoring people's appearance and lives."

5 A 'stone' with large owl-like black eyes and a pockmarked 'face' introduced himself as responsible for all laboratory studies and analyses. His/her name was Zoom. (Here it should be noted that the king could not guess who had these names — women or men. Or maybe they didn't have any division into female and male gender? But now the king didn't have time to puzzle over this question. The reasons why they gathered here were much more important.)

6 "I, Your Majesty, am an astrophysicist, a star master if I may say so. My name is Staer. My task is to find a wormhole in the universe and send the Antipodals' ship off to another galaxy. It's possible they will change their characters and will have a desire to do good, and this will be their purpose in life."

7 "And I'm Nuri, dear King Smelan, and we already know each other well. I am responsible for communication between superbiotechs and people. I'm an historian. I know many galaxies and have studied your Earth — its history and evolution."

Smelan already knew Nuri's voice and now he saw him a second time. He really liked the 'stone' like portrait of Nuri — it was, one could say, his friend, or so he felt.

Chapter 15

Ku swayed and drew Smelan's attention: "I will briefly report everything that has been done, and then you can ask us questions."

Smelan heard in turn from all members of the committee what had been done. And here are their reports:

1. An orbital ship with a scientific centre and laboratories were assembled.

2. A magnetic trap was created for the Antipodals' ship. It is completely neutralised for Earthlings. Time inside the ship is stopped. Staer has already discovered a so-called wormhole to another galaxy CT-13-13 with polar-opposite conditions of life and with another time dimension. It remains to obtain the king's consent to the deportation of the hostile ship from the solar system of the Milky Way galaxy, where the Earth is located.

In the galaxy, CT-13-13, the Antipodals will have a great chance to change for the better and turn into a positive force.

3. All scaly and infected people, turned into freaks, will remain paralysed for a while.

4. DNA of insects, birds, animals and plants has been defined from the specimen collected from the surface of the Earth. They had to do it in order to revive life on Earth.

5. The fact was established that superbiotechs are visible on the Earth in the spectrum of the sun, which differs from the wave 'climate' of Prima. This caused doubts about the idea of the existence of the Primleans on Earth in a parallel world. The visibility of the Primleans would disturb the habitual balance and evolution of Earthlings. Superbiotechs do not want to violate the evolutionary process — it is against the laws of the universe. They had to discuss this situation with the king.

6. Nuri had prepared ideas for the celebrations of Earthlings.

After a short pause, Smelan saw Ku sway slightly and heard his confident and calm voice: "Dear King Smelan, now you know what we have done during this month on Earth. We are ready now to hear your questions and suggestions. You are welcome."

As Smelan was so excited he couldn't say a word.

The familiar voice of Nuri led him out of numbness: "Dear Smelan, calm down. We are all here as your friends. I understand the importance of this meeting for you and your emotional state. But you must gather your thoughts. Remember the main exercise of yoga for relaxation — take a deep breath in three times slowly and then out — and all will be well."

Smelan immediately followed this advice and in fact quickly calmed down. He began by thanking the entire Star Committee once again, and asked them to pass his warmest gratitude to all Primleans.

Then he said: "Dear Primleans, I would like to invite you to stay on Earth, despite the fact that you are becoming visible in the solar radiation spectrum. Yes, it would be difficult to live in cities in a parallel dimension, since in the development of civilisation the Earthlings lag behind you, Primleans, by at least a million years. In other words, coexistence in populated areas of the Earth is unacceptable. This is unfortunate news, and I am very saddened. However, I have thought about it and it seems to me that I've found a solution to the problem.

"We have many vast deserts on Earth. People cannot live there — there is absolutely no rain, no water, no greenery or trees, and it is too hot for people; the temperature sometimes reaches sixty degrees. People never go there; they do not drive or fly there.

"But this climate for you, Primleans, would be suitable. Maybe you will consider this idea. You know that you will be more than welcome on our Earth. I assure you we will be happy to know that you are on Earth as our good neighbours and friends."

"Thank you, Smelan," Ay answered in a low voice. "We, all Primleans, will consider your proposal. We are used to living in higher temperatures, but perhaps our physicists will solve this problem. Please continue."

"I turn to point 2," the king continued. "I'm glad that Staer has found such a way to get rid of the Antipodal ship and even with the probability that they can become friendly subjects in the universe. Send them through the 'wormhole' into another galaxy. Thank you, Staer. And can I ask you what a 'wormhole' is? It sounds a bit peculiar..."

"The wormhole," answered the astrophysicist Staer, "explained simply, is a tunnel in your Milky Way galaxy, the shortest distance for a ship to reach another galaxy. This is not a straight line from point A to point B, but it reminds one of a wormhole with all sorts of twists and turns. Therefore, we astrophysicists jokingly called this indirect way a 'wormhole'."

"Oh, how interesting it all is! It is a pity that I'm not an astrophysicist, but I certainly, by all means, will now introduce this subject in schools. Let the children soon begin to understand the 'wormholes' and calculate the routes of spacecraft through the galaxies: so amazing, so interesting."

The king had a short respite, drank half a glass of water and continued in a cheerful, confident way:

"With your permission, dear Committee, I will move on to point 3. Could you, please, tell me briefly how all the 'scaly ones' and other freaks in just one day will turn into ordinary, normal people on each continent!"

Lol answered this question. She said that the superbiotechs had worked in the laboratory all this time and found a composition of bioradiation that would kill the viruses that infected people. After irradiating the continent, within one day people would return to their human form. Consciousness and ability to think would be cleared of weakness and confusion. Children and all people will stop doubting 'what is good and what is bad' Children and grown-ups will stop offending each other, fighting.

Fear, greed for money and gluttony will disappear in people. Humans will love each other, and never kill anyone. People will stop being drunkards and loafers. Never, ever again will people try to poison other people with illegal drugs, like they are rats. All drugs, which affect the health and ability to think clearly, will disappear forever. So such good, worthy beings will Earthlings become, quite the same as in God's view for mankind.

"It's amazing, I cannot even find words to express my gratitude to all of you," King Smelan exclaimed, deeply touched.

All the stone portraits swayed; Primleans were pleased to see how happy the king was to hear about the future of mankind.

"I have left for today the last small question to Nuri. What are your celebration ideas?" However, Nuri replied that this would be his beautiful and wonderful surprise for all the reborn Earthlings. He also said he knew how Earthlings loved surprises, and therefore wanted this to remain a surprise.

"So," Ay swayed, "for today, our meeting can be considered complete. Nuri will be in constant contact with you, King Smelan, and when necessary we will meet again and discuss the progress achieved. You have all worked very hard. Thank you, my friends.

"I wish all of you to achieve good results, which will be a reward for your conscientiousness."

His stone head swung and gradually melted into the air. The rest of the 'stone' portraits, too, slightly shaking as a sign of farewell, began to disappear into the air.

Chapter 16

Smelan was overexcited with the information and news, but he felt himself, as the saying goes, 'in the seventh heaven', although he really was in the seventh heaven, one can imagine. Nuri suggested walking the king to his cabin.

Once in the cabin, Smelan 'moved gently' to his favourite chair. He rejoiced in his heart, a smile did not leave his face.

"Well," he purred, everything goes according to the plan of the Primleans, and how quickly and accurately everything is performed! Supposing our people would work so well and smoothly on Earth — that is my dream. Aah, really there's nothing to blame my people for. They were good people and happy... but sometimes there were cases... oh, but one shouldn't now go back in time; I would be terribly glad to see them. It does not matter, small mistakes and blunders, everything will be forgiven. How I have missed people — my relatives, friends, and all mankind. We are very interesting and so different, so different. One person dreams of cows and chickens and yet another wants to draw the best picture in the world, and someone dreams about flights to the stars; so impossible to tell who's better... ah, and we are all good. All good diversity feeds our brains with interesting ideas and makes us dreamers."

Well, what about you, my friend, do you dream about anything?

"However, I now have a lot to do, and the sooner I manage it, the sooner I shall see my darling wife and daughter, and my friends. Back to work, Your Majesty," he said to himself.

The king had to continue preparation for the holiday as well as to think about where it would be best to put tents and how to feed people, while the superbiotechs set up farms, factories for food production, and also build up companies for the production of houses, cars, trains, airplanes and so on...

"So much work to do... How will I not get confused, and miss something important? Ah-hah, a plan, I need to just make a plan and pull myself together. When everything goes according to the plan, everything will be fine!" Smelan began to draw up a new plan.

"So," thought he, "first I need to talk to Nuri again. I will tell him about my different ideas for the celebrations. Secondly, we must together find places where the tents will be pitched. Third is to discuss the tube-food menu. Then, maybe, we will discuss the main industrial centres and farming areas.

"It's no joke to revive life on Earth and restore production, even partially, both agricultural and industrial. However, enough of being afraid, horrified and panicked. As the saying goes: 'fear has big eyes' and more: 'the eyes are afraid, but the hands are busy'. So here you are, hands, take over the job, and my head, too, don't lag behind," the king commanded himself.

Smelan thought about Nuri, and he soon appeared. "Greetings, Your Majesty, yes, you are right, we need to discuss many questions. Where do we start?"

Chapter 17

"Dear Nuri, I'm glad to welcome you too. I think we shall start with a map of the Earth and see where it is best to arrange villages. Then we need to discuss the tube — food for the regenerated Earthlings."

"Excellent. But before we begin to plan the location of the villages, I must tell you, Smelan, that the world population will be much smaller now. As I already mentioned, we will be able to revive only those of these 'scaly' freaks, who are still moving. According to our estimates, from the eight billion people there remain only a quarter, that is, two billion. We really can return them to a human appearance, and also we'll make them healthy. These people will begin to build a new life on Earth. Besides two billion are not so little for the Earth. I am sure they will work hard and will be able to restore life on Earth."

"It's wonderful," exclaimed the king. "Of course, I'm sorry for all the others who cannot be brought back to life, but if this is not possible, then we have to be reconciled with this, no matter how hard it may be. We must look to the future and move forward."

"You are absolutely right, Your Majesty, you cannot grieve forever about something that cannot be restored or corrected. We superbiotechs have already learned so to do. There's no point in wasting energy when with the help of this energy, you can do something good and useful.

"So back to the matter in hand. It seems to me that it would be possible to accommodate about half a billion on every continent. In Australia and South America, a little less, they are smaller than other continents, and besides there is a vast desert in Australia, and there are so many mountains in South America, so it will be difficult to organise villages for people. On the Euro-Asian continent it will be possible to build more towns, because this is a very large continent. Besides, I looked again at the map of the Earth, and maybe you will agree with me, dear Smelan, it will be better to set the small towns near the big rivers — people need water, a lot of water; and fields also need it for growing vegetables and grains and so on."

"Of course, Nuri, you're absolutely right. Everybody and everything needs a lot of water. Of course using deserts and mountains for towns is not a good idea. In deserts there is no water, and mountains are difficult to access and traverse.

"Besides, Nuri, I thought that there should be not only dwellings, but also schools for children, hospitals and gymnasiums for training in these little towns. Maybe you will say that it's a luxury now to be engaging in gymnastics but I don't think so. We people need to engage in physical exercises and do physical work to maintain good health. That's how the human body is built. We haven't reached your level yet — you do not need a muscular body, but we do. And, as the Romans used to say, 'a healthy mind in a healthy body', or in the original Latin, 'mens sana in corpore sano'."

"Yes, I agree with you, Your Majesty, that the human body needs physical activity so that it works well, and people are always in a good mood. However, in our circumstances, it will still be a luxury. After all, we need quickly, very quickly, to build simple houses for billions of people. So there will be more than enough of physical work; you can just imagine that you'll also need to work in the fields to grow grain, vegetables and fruit. In fact you won't be eating tube-food for the rest of your life, will you? It's only for emergencies. Besides one must build factories and plants to produce cars, trains, planes, televisions, and computers and so on, Your Majesty.

"There will be a lot of work, too much," Nuri added. "All will have enough physical exercise; choose any job you wish to, and you'll have no time at all to do acrobatics in the halls. You will build them much later, when you have free time for this, and much less work to do."

"Well, Nuri, you've convinced me completely," the king sighed.

Chapter 18

Having come to a common conclusion, Smelan and Nuri went into a detailed study of the map. They needed to choose rivers and the number of towns and how many people could live there. They also had to choose places for the towns. This work took almost a whole week. "If it were not for Nuri, who worked both day and night and made all the calculations in seconds, then for such a job," thought Smelan, "earthmen would have spent a year, or even more."

"Well, the plan is ready, dear King, it is time to start building. We will work through continent by continent. We will build towns on the continent, then restore the green blanket on this continent and then... and then free from the virus all those who were infected on that continent. After that, we will move to another continent and do the same there.

"I have a suggestion, to start with the least populated continent — Australia. Do you agree with me, Smelan?"

"Yes, OK. It is better to make the first steps with a less difficult continent. My head is spinning, and excitement overwhelms my heart. How it will all go and turn out!"

"Everything will be under our control, and we rarely make mistakes, umm... well, maybe once in a thousand years, not more often, so let's be positive, dear Smelan."

"Well, you've absolutely convinced me. Now I have a question: What kind of materials will you build houses from? I do not see any factories producing bricks or finished walls, or everything else that is needed to build houses."

"It is easy to answer this question. We will build houses from the air!"

"Er-m, how?" exclaimed an astonished Smelan.

"Just out of your air, because it has all the necessary elements for complex chemical compounds. Air consists of nitrogen, hydrogen, oxygen. We will add some silicon from the soil, and the strongest fabric for the house will be ready. Apart from this, air makes the best insulation, if you want to know. It would be good to use in the colder regions of the Earth. So you can better imagine it yourself, I can compare future houses with a bouncy castle in which children used to play.

"Only our houses will not bounce and nobody will jump in them. Although the house will be inflatable, it will be strong and stable. Everything will be ready inside in the way that people are used to. There will be bedrooms, living room, dining room, kitchen and bathroom. These houses will be single-storey, and therefore will need more land for their construction on Earth. However, there is enough space for everyone; your Earth is very large. A group of engineers and architects have already begun to design and manufacture this fabric for houses and draw up plans for different houses per person and per family."

"Such great news, you always go ahead of my questions," said Smelan. "I approve of all your ideas and plans, dear Nuri. Only one last question: do you not need to tell the Committee — CSE — before you start building houses so that they can approve your plans?"

"Worry not, Smelan, I'm in constant contact with Ku, chairman of the Committee for the rescue of the Earth and Issa, who is responsible for landscaping. I've also had a lot of conversations with Lol. Every day we discussed progress and problems and found the best solutions. I am fully responsible for the implementation of this part of the project on the Earth, and the Committee trusts me absolutely. I'm the coordinator and manager; I connect the different sections of the project.

"The construction of all 'tent' towns in Australia will take two to three weeks. After this, Issa with her group will take care of restoring plants and then biologists with Lol will start work. One day they will go out spraying gas to revitalise the paralysed 'scalies' and, without losing time they will then use another gas that will free all infected people from viruses. It will be a truly great day, the most important first step on the path to the rebirth of mankind.

"Then people will need to settle into houses. Lol, with a group of Primleans, will carry out this work in a few days. Also, TV will be set up to work in every house. There will be an announcement of your speech. People will be informed of the day, and the time and place of your address to the people. I think, Your Majesty, you need to be ready to meet people in twenty-seven to thirty days. While people wait for your speech on TV, we shall organise broadcast of historical and documentary programmes, so that people will know and recall their past, and see the tragedy that occurred on Earth. It will be a recovery period, though not a long one, until your speech. Then people will need to get to work.

"So, following your earthly calendar, it will take us about eight months to start and finish our project of saving the Earth on all continents. Then will come the year four thousand according to the earthly calendar, which will be significant for the Earth, and joyful, and will mark the beginning of a new life!

"After we restore Australia, we will take a tour and you will see everything with your own eyes. After that you can even stay there, if you wish. People will recognise you. Despite the tragedy on Earth you have lived on in folk tales of people who passed on your story — the flight of the King to God — from generation to generation. Your portraits hung in many houses, and on television until recently there were programs in which people tried to imagine what could possibly have happened to you. However, many believed in your return and God's help, despite there being no news from you for such a long time. Here you tell them (maybe at length) about all your adventures and travels."

"Oh, my imagination goes wild from your stories and suggestions, Nuri. Is it really in a month that I will see my dear people? My brains can hardly process this, but I believe every word you say."

"Yes, yes, everything will happen just like this. Now you'd better have a rest, Smelan; I can see you are too excited and have overworked your brain. I will make contact immediately with our technical team and we will begin to realise your dream, Your Majesty.

"Thank you from the bottom of my anguished heart and overexcited head. I am 'sailing' to my cabin to rest, think and dream."

"I'll be in touch, Your Majesty" Nuri stayed behind.

Chapter 19

King Smelan spent this month in routine — he wanted to strengthen his body, did exercises in the mornings, and afternoons practised yoga. Nuri visited the king from time to time, and they exchanged news — how things were going with the construction of houses for Earthlings, and what other new ideas Smelan had come up with for the celebrations. Time really didn't fly, but 'went unhurriedly' as it seemed to the king. However, he knew that one must have patience; and he was able to wait, as you know.

Then, finally, came the day of the excursion to Earth. Nuri appeared in the king's cabin on the eve of this day and announced the forthcoming excursion. Smelan was certainly waiting for this day, but when Nuri told him that tomorrow they were flying to the Earth, the brain in the king's head suddenly stalled and he was lost for words.

"Well, well, dear Smelan, I understand your excitement, but everything is going according to plan and everything will be fine. The houses are built; plenty of tube-food is delivered to all 'tent' towns. All scaly monsters were treated; biogas has been applied to get rid of viruses. The process was successful, and now there is not one freak — neither a bulbous, nor a scaly one — in all of Australia. They've disappeared forever. Now

Australia is inhabited by people, and only by people. It's true, they really wonder what happened; the nature of Australia has changed so much. Houses and streets have become unrecognisable, and typical cities have disappeared! Now they are all settled in the same-looking houses; someone provides them with tube-food. Every morning at every house, there appears a large box with tube-food and all sorts of drinks.

"No one remembers himself as a 'scaly freak', so there's a lot of talk and surprise. Here you tell them everything, everything that happened to you and about plans for the future. Above all, we checked their health, and found that they are practically all healthy — great news. 'What are they doing? you ask. They walk, talk, watch TV and exchange ideas, gathering together on lawns or by the sea. They have a recovery period now; it's better not to bother them. It turned out that many children were released from viruses. They are like normal children, play without a care, and in my opinion don't discuss anything, or worry about anything. Children tend to accept the conditions of their lives without question, whatever they may be. They do not criticise anything, but simply get on with life, and the main problem for them, it seems to me, is 'what game shall we play now or next?' So this is more good news — you have many children on Earth, which means that the Earth has a future, and it will grow from today. So, Your Majesty, your appearance and your story are very important. All adults and children should hear from you. Look what I've brought you."

The king opened the box and saw his royal earthly clothes, which he wore on the same day when he went to God... Smelan's eyes climbed on his forehead from astonishment. "You're a magician, Nuri!"

"We from Prima are all wizards, from your point of view. It takes too long to explain, dear Smelan; I still need to prepare the ship for tomorrow's excursion to Earth. So tomorrow morning you put on your usual royal clothes. People will recognise you right away. Well, until tomorrow, Your Majesty, and I wish you a good rest before the flight."

"My appreciation and enormous gratitude to you." whispered King Smelan, still recovering from embarrassment and surprise.

Chapter 20

It was March, 3099. The king got up very early, did the morning exercises, had a tube breakfast and drank coffee. He needed energy, so he did not deviate from the usual routine of the day. Then unhurriedly he put on his royal clothes. He has been caught with memories: his kingdom on the blossoming Earth, the good people which he loved with all his heart and all his soul.

After the long period of endless wars, peace had been achieved at last. Now all worked for the prosperity of the Earth and bold scientific ideas were becoming a reality. Along with the ground roads, city airways appeared. Along with the usual gardens, roof gardens had been set up on the houses. The children of these houses worked in the gardens. They took care of vegetables and fruit bushes — it was fun, and they liked being able to take to the school where they studied the harvest of fresh vegetables and fruits that they themselves had grown.

Everything, everything went well, until suddenly this invasion happened...

"But every new experience brings knowledge," thought the king. "After all, God and the superbiotechs told me that humanity suffered from imperfection of thoughts and from weak willpower. Mm-mm. We need to become stronger. We must learn to believe in ourselves and be able to say a loud NO to any bad habit, every bad idea. Oh, these harmful things, why do they sometimes cripple our lives? This must be stopped. This time the Primleans helped us, but we cannot hope every time for the help of aliens from the universe. It is necessary to try to make efforts to become invulnerable to any viruses. We must show the superbiotechs that we, too, are capable of..."

Nuri interrupted the thoughts of the king. It was exactly eight in the morning. His 'stony', handsome face appeared on the hologram. The first time Smelan saw an unusual 'face' as if to say, "well, well, Nuri was changing his appearance, he was different now, and had something earthly, I definitely could sense it."

"It's time, Your Majesty, and good morning to you. The ship's commander and the whole crew are ready to fly to Earth."

"I'm quite ready, dear Nuri."

"Yes, I see. You look great! So, shall we fly?"

"My greetings to you, Nuri. Yes, let us fly," whispered the king.

Chapter 21

Nuri guided their relaxed movement along the corridors. The walls glowed with a soft, greyish-bluish light. The silence of the space was broken by rare signals, sounding like melodic music and pleasant to the ear. As they moved along the corridor, the king began to notice the appearance on the walls of multi-coloured signals, as if running after them. They became more and more numerous. Smelan asked Nuri what these signals were, which had suddenly begun to appear. Nuri explained to the king that they were sensors in the walls to check the king's health before flying to the Earth. Smelan had to be absolutely healthy because he would have to endure great physical stress in this rocket. He had been in space for far too long and his muscles were accustomed to a complete lack of exercise. His body felt now like a light cloud, like fluff, but in the rocket and then on the ground it would regain weight, and he would feel how heavy it is.

"Well, so how is it?" asked the king. "Am I fit to survive the flight and then on the ground feel that I weigh seventy-seven kilograms? "

"Yes, dear Smelan. The sensors show that you are in good health, despite all the hardships of your journey. I must warn you that at first you will feel it's hard to move. You will feel that you are made of iron, but it will pass. Your body will get used to the gravity on the ground and will function normally."

Nuri stopped in front of a large oval door. A second later the door from the grey-blue became greenish and opened smoothly. They 'floated' into the rocket, which would take them to Earth.

Nuri showed the king to his chair. Smelan greeted the captain and the whole crew of the rocket although he didn't see anyone, but he knew that the entire team, including Captain Ay, and also Ku, Issa, Lol, the technical group and all the Primleans who wanted to visit the Earth, were there. The king thanked everyone for their invaluable assistance and interest in the Earth and Earthlings.

Nuri's voice was heard in the headphones; he said that the rocket was ready for launch, and Smelan needed to prepare for physical stress and overload. "The flight to the Earth will last only a few minutes, about eight minutes," he added. "If only Primleans were in the rocket, then the flight would last for several seconds, but you, Your Majesty need to adapt to gravity and therefore we will fly, one may say, with the brakes on, at Earth speed.

"Are you ready, Your Majesty, for the flight?"

"Yes," Smelan said shortly.

"Well, God be with us," thought Smelan out of habit.

The console seemed to come alive with numerous colour signals on the screen.

Smelan didn't feel the moment of separation of the rocket from the orbital station, but after a few seconds he started to feel heaviness in his body. The heaviness was growing quite rapidly; it was difficult for him to even move his fingers.

Nuri asked Smelan how he was.

"Thank you, Nuri, you are always very caring towards me. Yes, yes, you were right, I already feel that I'm not a cloud King... I'm as if all made of wood, maybe even iron... oh, I am heavy indeed, well, just like a stone King!"

"Don't thank me, dear Smelan, and don't worry, you will soon adapt to your weight and will feel fine in a day or two. By the way, look out of the illuminator."

With difficulty the king turned his head and saw that his blue Earth was approaching rapidly, and literally a minute later, he had already started to distinguish lakes, mountains, green forests, meadows and snaking rivers. The king's heart pounded, it rejoiced.

"Lord, I thank you for everything, for everything! You gave me such a good advice, and I found kind friends in the universe. They will return life to the Earth and human appearance to all people." Nuri's hologram appeared. "We'll be landing soon, Your Majesty."

The king did not feel any landing force, but again heard Nuri's voice: "Dear Smelan, we've landed, you are on the ground. Our common serious mission has come true!"

Chapter 22

"Here it is, this moment! It is done! I'm on the ground, on Earth!"

Smelan was so delirious with happiness that for the first time he didn't hear Nuri's voice. Nuri waited, he understood that the king needed to find his feet if he was to realise and feel this turning point in the history of the Earth and humanity. Ten minutes later, Nuri turned again to the king. He rang the bell that the king used in the palace when he had to call someone. This time such a familiar and earthly sound attracted the attention of the king, and he heard Nuri's voice. He suggested that he should not leave the rocket immediately, but calm down and put his thoughts and emotions in order. Also, his body had to get used to the Earth's gravity.

"Yes, yes," answered Smelan, "I fully agree with you. I feel completely overwhelmed, as if a huge tsunami had dragged me along the seabed, but I'm still alive..."

Or maybe it was an endless, adventure-crammed incredible dream? The thought swept through his head. He both believed and did not believe in what had happened to him, it was very much like the inventions of authors and storytellers. He decided to pinch himself and make sure he was alive and he was on the Earth. The king immediately did this.

"I'm alive, alive! I feel my heavy body, not my cloudy and weightless one. Great, tra-la-la!" However, when Smelan wanted to warm up, it was difficult. His body did not obey, it felt petrified. It was hard work to lift his arms or move his legs. His hands were like logs, and his legs were like an elephant's legs. Smelan looked around in bewilderment. "Well, well, calm down, calm down," he whispered to himself. "This is after all the gravity of the Earth; my dear Earth loves me, that is why she is pulling me in her direction with incredible strength. She also missed me, as well as I missed her. I have to wait a bit, my body will feel fine, and that is what Nuri said."

As always, Nuri's amusing and kindly head appeared on the hologram in the air.

"You are absolutely right, Your Majesty, don't worry. Yes, it will be difficult, I warned you, but it will pass. Now I've brought you a chair on wheels, and we can roll to the elevator."

"My caring friend. Thank you."

Smelan moved from the cosmonaut's chair to the wheelchair which rolled him up to the elevator. In less than two or three seconds Smelan and now visible Nuri were already on the ground.

"Are you ready, Your Majesty?"

"Yes," whispered the king.

Chapter 23

When the elevator door opened, sunlight hit the king's eyes. He squeezed his eyes shut. His eyes had forgotten how bright sunshine can be. He took a deep breath of the Earth's air and half-whispered half-sang:

— Hello, dear sun!

— Hello, my sweet native land!

— Hello, gorgeous meadows

— I'm happy to be in my homeland. I went away from you, I flew for so long, but now I'm back to you... forever!

Nuri appeared next to him. He was completely visible in the sunlight. He had the figure of a three-dimensional star with unequal rays. He barely touched the ground, jumping and moving in all directions. He arranged for the king a temporary house on the lawn, at the edge of the forest near the lake. The house was inflatable, and Nuri erected it right before the king's eyes. He invited Smelan to come in and see his new earthly dwelling.

Now the king could move a little. The arms and legs seemed a little lighter. He entered the house and was amazed at how comfortable it was, how bright and cosy inside. Everything that one needed was there: a living room, a dining room, a kitchen, and two bedrooms with a bathroom. The nature around the house reminded him of his royal garden.

Smelan was a humble king; he did not have 'a plethora of everything', there were not hundreds of bedrooms and ten dining rooms and living rooms — he did not need them. He believed that even though he was a king, he must have and use only what he needed. So this cute little house touched his heart immediately.

Smelan thanked Nuri, who settled himself into an armchair in the living room. The chair started to crackle and melt away little by little from the temperature of the 'star body' of Nuri. Smoke wafted into the air, and although the king had the most excellent manners and never pointed a finger at anyone telling them what to do and what not to do, even he had to invite Nuri to get out of the chair.

"Nuri," exclaimed Smelan, "our new house will burn like a match in no time if you do not rise from the chair. You are radiating heat, and the armchair twinkles like a Christmas tree."

"You worry in vain, Your Majesty, it will smoke a little and stop. "All the furniture and the house are made of materials which are not afraid of any temperature and will never catch fire — well, let's say, even five hundred degrees will not cause any danger."

"Excuse me, Nuri, I did not know that such heat-resistant houses and materials existed. We've had fires often, so I was so worried."

"Your Majesty, I invite you to rest. Choose yourself a comfortable chair. Now you will have your cup of coffee. Lunch will be later, after our conversation."

Nuri offered to discuss the plan of action for the next two or three days, and also for a week and a

month ahead.

"Yes, of course, Nuri. You are absolutely right. We need to decide what to do first, and what can wait."

So the king fell into the armchair feeling great pleasure; the armchair was so comfortable and smelled so deliciously of familiar plants that the king had to pinch himself so as not to doze off and get lost in a dream. He needed to keep his spirit and mind sharp.

PART THREE

Chapter 1

In the new house at the edge of the forest the king and Nuri prepared themselves to discuss what needed to be done. Nuri was right; his chair did not catch fire and even stopped smoking, despite the glow of his 'star body'.

Smelan was eager to meet people as soon as possible and talk, talk and talk some more with them. However, Nuri noted that first he needed to adapt, and that takes some time.

"I would like to tell you now, Your Majesty, what we have done, here, in Australia and then we can discuss further steps."

"Yes, yes, please do, dear Nuri, I am all ears."

"In brief we built houses for all the population in the most attractive areas of Australia. We eliminated all infected creatures and restored people to their normal appearance. They are now healthy and content; they are recovering, and observation shows that they are doing fine. The green world — grass and flowers, bushes and trees etc. — has been restored. Most animals have been revived. We installed TV broadcasting in every town, in every house. Now, Your Majesty, when you are ready to go to meet the people and have your speech and story to tell, we will fly to the capital of Australia, and there in the central square you will hold this gathering of the revived people. Your meeting will be broadcast to every town and the people can watch it on TV."

"Dear Nuri, I'm ready. I've prepared myself; everything is in my head and in my heart."

"Excellent, Your Majesty, and then we go the day after tomorrow. It will be Monday when people used to start the new week and make new commitments. You like Mondays, don't you?"

"Well, not always and not everybody does," smiled the king. "We people are not that predictable... sometimes singers for example like to start their tours and sing new songs on Fridays. However generally speaking you are right and it'll be a good day for us to start a new week, to make the first steps towards a new life on Earth. Thank you, Nuri, very much. I'm delighted to know that I shall see my people, thousands of them, so soon."

"Good, that's settled. So till Monday then," said Nuri. "Have a very good rest and accumulate more energy. I've left for you here special natural herbs which will boost your energy to the highest possible level for humans. Good night, honourable King."

"Wait, wait, please," hurried the king. "Where are you going to stay? Where are you going to sleep? You are very welcome to stay in this cosy house; you know this, don't you? I'll be very happy to share it with you."

"Thank you, dear King, you know we don't need to sleep and to get our energy from resting at night. We are working all the time or doing things we like to do, we have hobbies. We can easily recharge ourselves from the energy of the sun."

"Oh, how different you are! I can't really imagine that we'll be like this in a million years; Okay then, see you on Monday morning. You said we fly to the capital of Australia. Is it still Sydney or Melbourne?"

"It's Canberra, Your Majesty, and it's not far from here. I'll accompany you in a small jet craft. We'll be there in no time."

"And when do you think we'll return?"

"The same day, afternoon. I think it'll be better that way. You'll be very excited and tired. The meeting is expected to be emotional and after that you will definitely need a rest. It will take only half an hour to come back by jet. In a day or two we are flying to another continent. I have some more news to tell you, but maybe it'll be better to save it for after you see your people."

"What is it about?"

"It's about the Committee on the orbital station and some of their decisions."

"It's important, Nuri. Why don't you tell me now? I really don't mind talking more, it's not too late."

"All right then. First of all, the work on assembling the station from our prima ships is complete. Now the station is fully functioning, quite a powerful high-tech space mega craft. It'll stay in orbit at least another thousand years. It will be served by the team of Primleans and it will protect the Earth from some unexpected misfortune — asteroid impact or Antipodal attack or whatever space may throw at you.

"The second news — a large group of Primleans are going back to Prima, in fact most of them. They are concerned about the prospect of living in deserts and about being visible on Earth. Also, they don't think these restrictions of movement will suit them. They would prefer a total freedom of movement all over the planet because the speed of their movement is quite high and the deserts will be felt by them as a very limited living space.

"This is unfortunate. However, a lot of Primleans are staying here for longer — you know some of them: Issa, Lol, Hier, myself and Ku of course. I think we'll be visiting your deserts and spending some time in the orbital station. We still have a number of ships — at the moment they are orbiting Earth. We can use them to go for excursions to neighbouring galaxies, to explore and to find good living conditions for Primleans. Ay will go — he's the captain, the head of the ship's navigation team, and he has to go. Staer will take his position here, on the Earth orbital megacraft."

"Well, well what sad news. It's quite an unexpected development. I'm sure I must respect their decision. Everybody, including Primleans, I believe do what they think is right and good for them unless of course it makes others uncomfortable. I agree with you, dear Nuri, that their decision will not make our life less content. You've helped us a great deal, you saved us, you saved life on Earth, and now it's up to ourselves to try our best to be good, to do the right thing. Besides you say that quite a lot of Primleans are still staying with us. So in an emergency I suppose we can still seek a bit of advice from Primleans."

"Absolutely, no doubt about that. OK then, I am glad to hear that you are not upset or frustrated."

"Oh no. All what I feel is boundless gratitude to you, to Primleans, which will last forever."

"Excellent, Your Majesty. Now we have to decide whether you fly back to the orbital station to see the Committee before the Primleans return to Prima. However, I can organise broadcasting and you can talk to all those not leaving Earth, your house. If you want to know my opinion, I believe it would be better, because physically you are not as strong as we are: sorry to tell you this but we have to be practical now. So you'll save a lot of energy staying on Earth and talking to them via the satellite system."

"It's good, Nuri, I'll follow your advice, you've proved to me you are always right, the perfect Primlean,", smiled the king.

"Right, you will talk to the Committee via satellite after you meet the people. This meeting will be broadcast and the Committee will see and hear everything that will happen here on Earth. So, at your service, Your Majesty, everything is sorted and now I am leaving you. Have a pleasant evening and a good night's sleep.

"By the way, the TV satellite system is already set in every town and in every house. So you can watch the programmes — documentaries, programmes for children, and listen to some music and so on. I would be interested to know what you think about our choice of broadcasting."

"Thank you, Nuri and good night to you, whatever that means," smiled the king. I will definitely watch TV; it's such a good idea, and tell you later what I think."

Lightly jumping and hopping on his three star legs Nuri left the house.

Chapter 2

The whole of the next day the king spent alone. Nuri did not want to disturb him. He anticipated that Smelan had to contemplate and prepare himself to meet a large crowd of people. It would be very emotional for him and for the people as well.

The king got up early as usual, followed by morning exercises and breakfast. Then he was curious about the broadcasting on TV and touched the button Nuri had showed him.

Smelan made himself comfortable in the armchair and looked at the big screen. It was a film for children. The film was animated and the characters were very funny and jolly. He recognised some of them from the good old days on Earth, before his travelling to God.

Smelan was amazed at how the Primleans had made this film, which was so much like peoples' movies made by humans. "But they are Primleans and I'd better stop wondering every time. They are just wizards, magicians, enchanters," smiled the king to himself.

After a while he changed the programme and it was a documentary. It was about the time when he left the Earth travelling to God to seek help. He saw the crowd of people looking in the sky; he saw worried and hopeful faces. Then he saw Prima, but it was like a flickering screen, all the time changing colours and movement of little satellites around Prima. There was a short narrative explaining about the star Prima. Then again it showed briefly his return journey and in the end the voice of Nuri announced about the meeting in Canberra.

King Smelan would see people and tell them everything about his journey. He would have a chat with people and they could ask him any questions. Everybody would be very welcome to come. At the end the king would announce the days of weekly celebration over the whole Earth. The meeting would take place at:

Freedom Square, on Monday at ten o'clock in the morning.

After that day King Smelan and Primleans would start another cycle from the very beginning on another continent.

Now Smelan knew that people would have some information from TV, not in detail but generally they would know what had happened on Earth and some ideas about his journey. His role would be to fill the gaps with details and complete the whole picture — make it a masterpiece.

He worked very hard and by evening the speech was completed. He thought he had covered everything and was pleased with the result. Smelan had a light snack, listened to some favourite music from the good old days which brought peace to his mind and went to his comfy bed feeling excited in a good way, smiling to himself in anticipation of seeing people tomorrow at last. He was confident and calm. "Everything will be fine," he kept saying to himself, "and God be with me."

He fell asleep as soon as he touched the pillow with a happy smile on his lips.

Chapter 3

So, the morning had arrived, the great morning in his life and in the life of Earthlings and Earth.

Smelan got up early, and made breakfast for first time since he left Earth — his favourite, 'travelling cup' of coffee and the tube-spread tasting like wonderful strawberry jam on a piece of toast and even two real eggs. There were not any real fruits because fruit trees planted by the Primleans were still very young, but there were real eggs! It meant that chickens in the king's garden were already doing their job — laying very tasty eggs. It was a delicious and very earthly breakfast.

The king switched on the music, and started to dress himself, all in ceremonial clothes. He managed well and, as soon as he had finished, Nuri appeared. "Nuri always knows when to appear, not too early and not too late," the thought flicked through the king's head. "They never make an awkward appearance. Oh Primleans, Primleans..."

"Good morning, dear Smelan. I hope you had a good night's sleep and a wonderful earthly breakfast."

"Good morning, Nuri. Yes, indeed, I had a very tasty breakfast which I used to have back in the good old times, before travelling to Prima, couldn't be better. Now I am ready to go to meet people."

"Excellent, Your Majesty, the jet is near the woodland waiting for us; can we leave now, Your Majesty?"

"Of course," answered the king with a smile. He felt more and more bonds with Earth, with his suffering but sweet home.

King Smelan and Nuri left the house, crossed the green meadow full of pretty wild flowers and settled in the jet. Never before had Smelan seen such an odd-looking flying craft. The shape reminded him of a beautiful dragonfly. The wings were translucent with a lot of silvery, metallic, sparkling lines crossing them in a bendy way. Its body was long and elegant, and especially with these sparkling lines. Smelan decided not to ask about the appearance of the jet and all these shiny lines he was intrigued about. "I have to concentrate now on the meeting with people and shouldn't involve myself in a destructive conversation," he thought. It was very comfortable inside and felt somehow very calm.

Chapter 4

In no time at all they had arrived at Canberra and landed close to the main square.

King Smelan felt dizzy from excitement and not knowing what to expect, but he was the king; he must be calm and show a smiling face. So, before leaving the jet, he did a breathing exercise and said a short prayer: "God be with me," he whispered.

He was ready to appear out of the jet door.

The King stepped out. He saw people, people everywhere, thousands and thousands of them. They looked like ordinary people, nothing alien about them. Phew... it was a huge relief. The crowd was silent; this Smelan didn't expect to happen. He thought the people would be shouting for joy, singing, dancing, being excited, but nothing of the kind was happening. People were looking at him seriously; one could read attention and curiosity on their faces but definitely not a shred of any strong emotions showing excitement and rejoicing at this remarkable moment.

For a second King Smelan felt lost, but it wasn't the time to lose control of the plot. He pulled himself together and started his speech. After a while not much had changed. The expression on the faces was showing a great deal of interest, they were focused but still somehow distant as the king saw it. He didn't feel a connection with this huge crowd of people. He felt as though he was just their guest and not their dear long-awaited King.

The speech was long because obviously Smelan had so much to tell. However, people were attentive all the way through and didn't show any sign of tiredness, impatience or boredom.

When Smelan had finished there was no customary 'hurray' or applause — the crowd was mysteriously quiet. No questions, nothing. The King was close to losing control and becoming upset; all that he managed to do was to thank the people for coming and announce the celebration on Earth when all continents would be ready to do take part.

Smelan was confused, taken aback, baffled. He couldn't explain it and felt heartbroken. He had nearly turned round to go back to the jet but suddenly saw Nuri who had positioned himself several metres away from the stage. Being upset the king had forgotten to introduce the Primleans — some of whom had come especially to this meeting to be introduced by the king.

So he turned back to the people who were still standing patiently and looking at him. He waved his hand attracting attention and announced a short break after which he would introduce the group of aliens — the superbiotechs from the star Prima, who had helped the Earthlings and Earth.

Smelan stepped back into the shadow where Nuri had comfortably placed all his three legs. Nuri turned to the king and asked him to calm down, everything was going as it should be and the strange behaviour of the people was not strange at all but he would explain it later after the meeting. "Now, Your Majesty, please, be in good spirit. Your people love you and follow you but they have changed a bit, and their behaviour has changed too. There's a reason for this. In two minutes, it's not easy to tell everything about the treatment we gave them and how it affected their DNA. I repeat, we'll talk about it later. Now stop worrying and introduce us. There are three of us: Ay, the captain, me, the coordinator of the project and Lol, the scientist, who is responsible for the revival of the people. Well, we are ready to communicate with the people and show ourselves."

Chapter 5

It was a hot sunny day. Blue sky stretched to the horizon with not a cloud. King Smelan announced the introduction of the superbiotechs not on hologram but alive as they were.

First Nuri appeared. In perfect English, slightly rocking on his three legs, he introduced himself and, together with the king, related briefly what they had done and what they were going to do. For more information and full details, he advised the people to watch TV. People started smiling!

"Uh, oh," thought the king. "What's happening? Why do they start smiling now?"

"And now," continued Nuri, "our captain and scientist from Prima are coming to you with their greetings. Look they are approaching."

The people suddenly saw the dragon-like jet making a vertical landing near the square. Two superbiotechs disembarked and, bouncing like balloons, quickly reached the podium. But as soon as they approached the stage, they looked different, not like balloons at all, and the colour of their silhouettes was different too. Silvery/gold/copper colours reflected by the sun made them appear very sparkly and dazzlingly bright. But what was amazing was the changing of colour and shape with every slight movement. The spectacle was hypnotic and without any reason —

from the king's point of view — the people started smiling again and looking at each other, saying something, maybe exchanging opinions. He saw jolly faces, and again for him it was a mystery.

"Why are the people smiling now but not when I was greeting them and making a speech?" he wondered. "Well, well, Nuri will explain this to me I hope."

Meanwhile the prickly-looking Primlean had made a quick change of his appearance and the crowd became very quiet. He introduced himself as the captain of the Primleans' spaceship, and all his tentacles became dark grey, looking very serious. While he was talking — again in perfect English — his colour and the shape of his 'body' had changed several times and it was very entertaining not only listening to him but watching these mesmerising changes as well.

Ay said that now the process of restoring life on Earth had started and had been completed in Australia. After all the continents had their normality back, they would feel they had done everything to restore life on Earth. The Primleans would then return to their star Prima and a little group of Primleans would remain on Earth, as they had discussed with King Smelan.

As they already knew, Earthlings had been the victims of this attack and now Primlean scientists would send the antipodal ship through the 'wormhole' into a different galaxy.

Earth would be free from invaders, would be protected for another million years by a Primlean ship which would be in orbit providing bioenergetic protection. He was sure in one million years' time they would find a way to protect themselves from destructive invaders. Maybe Primleans would find a suitable star for them in the Milky Way galaxy and then they would all be good friendly neighbours.

"I wish you all to enjoy your revival and I give thanks to God and you, great, brave and loving King Smelan. Without you Earth would be a dead object in space now."

Making himself greenish-bluish and moving all his tentacles on the top of his 'body', he hopped off.

Next Lol appeared. The shape and colour of her silhouette was intricate too and, with every movement it kept changing its appearance as with the other superbiotechs.

She told briefly about the project of reviving the Earthlings on each continent and mentioned that from now on the people would be stronger in their minds and each person would be able to resist any wrongdoing, even in small matters. She sent to the crowd a flickering cloud of lights and disappeared.

Now Smelan announced the end of the meeting. People could obtain more information from regular TV programmes, and from now on there would be a special programme with updates of what was happening on each continent. He was smiling broadly and wished all the people an interesting and satisfying life. Accompanied by Nuri they went to the jet.

Chapter 6

"Well, well," the king sighed when he and Nuri returned to the king's new home.

"Nuri, you wanted to tell me something important and explain the strange, from my point of view, behaviour of the people in the meeting. I naturally expected the people would be excited to see me after all this horror happened to them and to Earth. But they were quiet and serious-looking — no overwhelming emotions."

"Yes, Your Majesty, you are right in your observation. The people were quiet because from now on they have a slightly different genetic make-up."

"What do you mean? Are they human? They are not half robots, are they?"

"No, they are not but they will be much less emotional and much more sensible, analytical, reasonable. It's because, when we revived them, we used our traditional technique of medical restoration, which totally recovers the 'system' — I mean human body — and restores it to perfection. Perfection from our point of view means seeing, hearing, feeling, then analysing your sensors and sending them along via the correct route in your brain. As you know, the brain is a very complicated organ and it has a billion different interconnections, so that it works perfectly when the right connection is chosen.

"All mistakes and errors are history now in all rejuvenated, inspired people. Now they are accomplished. They will not suffer any more in their lives because their choice will be always one hundred percent right. Don't you think, Smelan, that it is good for people?"

"Oh yes, sure, Nuri. I'm glad they'll be better, actually perfect in their minds. I hope it will make their lives happier, filled with different interests and occupations. However, I am different, and I am not perfect! Do you think that communication between us will be broken, lost?"

"It might happen to some degree. But we couldn't have done it differently because of the fragility of your brains. Now you have quite a difficult task: on one side all the recovered people are not fragile in their brains any more, they are very analytical, with common sense in their behaviour, and, I am afraid I have to say this, they are more advanced than people you remember. So you, Your Majesty, have to catch up! But don't you worry, we can help you, we can, as it were, 'rewire' your brains. That is the main thing I wanted to talk about. Do you want to be a bit different, more advanced and to better understand contemporary people?"

"Nuri, it's such life-changing news. I have to think about it...what about my relatives — my daughter, my wife and close friends? Will they have to be modified too?"

"Yes, Smelan, of course you have to think, I won't rush you now. If you decide to go ahead with the transformation, then your relatives will take the same course — they can't be left far behind the other people. How long do you think it will take you to come to a decision?"

"I will be ready to give you the answer tomorrow morning."

"Excellent, Your Majesty. Now have a good rest. You've had a very eventful day. I will see you tomorrow then."

"Yes, my head is spinning again. I have to do a lot of thinking. Thank you, Nuri, for everything, for your immense and extensive help, and conducting and organising the meeting. See you tomorrow."

The king dropped into his favourite armchair and fell into thought. It was a lot to contemplate and imagine how you can become different; the different way of thinking is like having somebody else's head on your shoulders. Forget your own brain and reset it with a more perfect Primlean one! The King felt very uncomfortable; he was struck dumb by this idea.

Chapter 7

The evening was disappearing fast and Smelan still had no idea what to decide. He asked God to help him in his usual evening prayer and then he just sat and waited for God's sign.

God appeared quite soon in the form of thoughts. Smelan 'heard' him saying:

"I understand your difficulties in taking this particular decision. In your mind you follow the ancient and fundamental belief that God is the Creator and He always knows what he is doing. I agree with you. That is so. Besides, I think you and your family and friends, who are still on their way to be recovered, had better keep this way of thinking and believing because nothing and no one can be more than Creator.

"Yes, the Primlean was correct — reanimated people will be different and technically more advanced compared with you but they will not be as complete as you are in your old ways. They will be lacking these good old elements of personality like humour and laughter, which you have and your descendants will always have. Strange it might sound, but even imperfection can sometimes show more genius than square perfect heads of 'new' people, because your brains are boundlessly creative and unpredictable — even for me, he-he-he! So I find the evolution of unpredictable people much more interesting than the predictable development which Primleans offered you."

"My God, what you are saying is indisputably true, but you see what has happened to us when human beings have these unpredictable brains. We can make mistakes — insignificant ones and huge, life-changing ones. Without you and Primleans, humanity would have disappeared by now!"

"I understand your worries and you are right — wrong thinking can take you to a land of troubles with a rather horrible ending. But that is how you will learn from your mistakes and then strive to achieve a better life. This learning process with mistakes and recovering and standing on your feet again I call life — the Life I gave to people on Earth.

"I think it is interesting to explore, create, make mistakes, then stand on your feet again, fight for a better life, feel that you CAN DO many things, feel power within yourself. Isn't that exciting? Worth living for?"

"Yes, inspiring" sighed the king. "My God you're very convincing and I'll follow your advice. I like it very much, I'll remain and be myself, good or at times not perfect, but myself. It's a freedom to be who you are, it's a fantastic feeling! Thank you, my Lord!"

"Peace be with you, in your head and in your heart. Brave, big-hearted and honourable Smelan. I like you, my creation, and dear humans."

Chapter 8

The king rubbed his eyes and patted his cheeks.

"What a strange dream I had last night! But so clear, so clear! Like I talked to God and he answered my questions... actually I feel now that I have come to a conclusion of what to do and my answer for Nuri is now ready. Ah hah, miracles can happen, not only on Prima star but sometimes here, on Earth... hmmm... what a beautiful night I had."

Smelan did his morning exercises and started to make breakfast. He sang to himself quietly and felt very cheerful. His favourite cup of coffee was ready and he had it with an apple mush on toast. Now a cup of coffee didn't flow to him like on Prima star or in the orbital station. Now he had to do it himself. Smelan didn't mind, he was quite a capable king — not a sissy.

He sat in his armchair and recalled again his dream. Yes, all was clear for him now and he was ready to talk to Nuri. Of course Nuri appeared as soon as Smelan thought he was ready.

"Good morning Smelan. Did you sleep well last night?" He placed all his legs comfortably on another armchair.

"Very well, thank you, dear Nuri. I can tell you more, so much that now I am totally sure what I would like to do and, more accurately, what I don't want to do."

"Let me guess, Smelan. I like this little game with you. Give me five seconds."

"I am very generous, you know, and I can give you five minutes."

"I don't need five minutes and I can tell you now that you have decided not to take our advanced method of transforming the mind. Is that so?"

"Exactly, my dear friend. I have decided to be as I am — no more and no less. I can tell you more: I have decided that all my relatives and friends will not take it either. We will be the group of old-fashioned humans — good golden antiquity — and stay this way until somebody marries a 'new' person. Then it will be a mixture of human being genes and who knows... maybe it will be very interesting?

"I know, I know you might say that imperfection of thinking brought us to the edge of extinction. I hope not. Actually, I know that we are a group of good people; we are not corrupted, neither liars nor cheats nor violent. In short, we are physically and mentally healthy so there is no risk involved. So what do you think, my dear Nuri?"

"Well, well, Smelan. I really didn't expect this. I was sure you would rush to new technology but I totally respect your choice and I think it's really the king's choice. Remain as you are because you are the top rank of the human race indeed. Sorry to praise you — who am I to judge the king — but you are to collect the best words which exist in your language. So that's settled. Excellent. Now we have to decide what continent will be next to do the job."

"Africa, I think," replied the king.

"Good. It'll take me a day to prepare our journey and we fly by jet the day after tomorrow."

Chapter 9

Smelan spent the next day contemplating what he saw and felt about the 'new' people. He watched this meeting again on TV.

"Well, well, now I understand why the people were serious and quiet with contemplative faces. They felt more 'at home' when they saw Primleans. They have something from Primleans' DNA, they are kind of their 'children', their creations and they felt it somehow! Wow, what a discovery I have made; and, for some reason, I'm sure it is the truth. That's why Nuri didn't tell me anything about their smiling, maybe he didn't want to upset me? Or... why? I have to ask him directly.

"Well, any way you can't make people love you, one must deserve it. So I have to start from the very beginning and do my job for people whom I love and will do everything in my power to make them content. And then, as they say, 'what will be, will be'," smiled the king to himself. "Now I have to accept the situation without any sorrow. It will be all right, I have to believe in it.

"However, it's time to prepare myself and the luggage for tomorrow's journey. We go to Africa to revive people and then to South and North America, and then to the biggest and the last destination — the Eurasia continent.

"There my dearest family and friends will be revived and I will see them at last. Oh, what a day, what a great moment it will be. I have been waiting for this day for such a long, long time, not only waiting but I have been fighting for this day, and have done all that I possibly could to meet my dearest ones."

All went well on other continents like in Australia, and at last Nuri and Smelan landed in the Eurasia continent. It was the first week of December in the year 3099.

Chapter 10

The green meadow and hills stretched to the far horizon. It was nostalgically a dear landscape. The King closed his eyes and took a deep breath. "Good Lord, I am at home!" It was sunny, silent, pleasurable. One could hear only the gentle wind playing with long grasses of the meadow.

They were near the former capital of the kingdom, the city by name Semper. There, about twenty kilometres to the south of the city, in the big pyramid, were put to rest his family and friends. Nuri had told him about it. Primleans searched the continent with high tech. equipment and found the place of rest. In fact, it was inside the rocky mountain called Zarya.

The King was very upset but didn't allow himself to be caught up by grief. It was the last marathon for him and he had to accomplish it.

So they had three weeks left before Christmas. The time for completion of the project on Earth was coming to an end. The King, Nuri and other Primleans had to finish the great animation of the people. Then grandiose celebrations over the whole Earth would start on Christmas Eve and last until New Year 4000 and maybe a bit longer. That was the plan.

"A lot to do," said Nuri in the morning to the king, stepping into the house. "What do you people say: 'Roll up your sleeves'?"

"Exactly, my dear Nuri, you are a good student and have learned not only perfect English but colloquial phrases too," smiled the king.

"Well, well, soon after all this will come your great long-awaited moment — we bring back to life your daughter and wife and relatives and friends. They will be surrounded by people and the green world and it will not be traumatic for them at all. They will be just a bit surprised and confused but then it will be your job to tell them all your stories. How does that sound?"

"It sounds Godly, magical, amazing and happy!"

"So here we are, back to work. You know what to do today, don't you?"

"Yes, I do indeed: prepare my speech. I actually have to do very few changes, just change the name of the continent and some other little details."

"How about mentioning meeting with the Royal family several days later? Do you call that 'other little details'?"

"No, of course not. I actually wanted to ask you when exactly my family will be brought back to life."

"Let me see. This continent is huge, vast. It will take longer to do each leg of the project. We have already started and done something: sprayed gas and paralysed the scalies; also brought the green world back to life. Now we have to set up towns and organise tube-food delivery on a regular basis to each house. Then comes the stage of reviving and rejuvenating people, not all of them, as I told you, but still millions of them. Well, we will accomplish this project by eighteenth of December.

"Shall we then let the people get accustomed to the surrounding buildings and learn from TV, in short, what has happened to Earth"

"Sure, I think it's a good idea. How about my speech?"

"Your Majesty, maybe first you should meet your family and friends and then come to the people all together and make the speech. Would you like that?"

"Nuri, it would be absolutely wonderful! Much better than me alone and lonely, standing in front of the people. No doubt. I totally agree with your brilliant idea."

"Good, then all you have to do, Smelan, is relax; watch TV about the work we have done on all continents. You didn't have much time to do it before, we were so busy.

Listen to your favourite music, practise some cooking, write your memoir at last... well, you know best what you can do, you are the king!"

"You are right, my dear friend. I know what I should do. I will be in touch with all other continents and the committees which are to organise the great celebration on Earth. We have to discuss the progress they have made."

"Splendid, your Majesty! You can do it now without leaving the house; all the satellite system is in operation.

"I'll go now and from time to time I'll come and see you. If you need me, just think of me and I will come — you know this, don't you?"

"Yes, yes, thank you, dear Nuri. I wish you well and success in your honourable execution."

Chapter 11

The days flew fast and Nuri popped in one evening to tell the king that now he could move from the contemporary little house to his new big royal dwelling. Smelan was on cloud nine!

In his new palace the king lost no time. He went upstairs to his mini-communication centre, which Nuri had organised for him, and started to call the different continents, all six of them, to discuss the stage of preparation for the celebration over the whole Earth. He managed to do it rather quickly because it appeared that people of all continents were so enthusiastic, and energetic, and spirited. They had worked so tirelessly all this time that they had nearly accomplished the preparation.

It was a rather big and pleasant surprise for the king. So the Gala was ready to get up steam on all continents and the committees were just waiting for the date to start the head-spinning celebrations. The King was delighted indeed. Now, after all, these mighty efforts were coming to the end.

He went to bed tired but with the happy smile of a person who has reached the 'summit'. Smelan could now expect the meeting with his long-missed wife and daughter and friends shortly. But every time when he imagined seeing them after all this time, he felt his feet getting wobbly, his lips trembling, and his eyes moistening.

"I have to calm down," he kept repeating to himself, "and prepare myself. I am the king; I can keep my emotions hidden and my face happy. I have to be the jolly King and not 'a leaf trembling in the wind'."

"What can I do... what can I do to help myself? Come on, Smelan... I have to meditate and breathe in, and breathe out..." Smelan talked to himself out loud. He found the little rug, put it on the floor and started to do yoga.

After half an hour he felt much stronger emotionally, and decided he had to do yoga three times a day before seeing the relatives.

"Now I have time to listen to some music and watch TV. I think tomorrow I'll meet Nuri and tell him that I'm ready to meet my family."

Chapter 12

Nuri appeared in the morning after the king had finished breakfast.

"Good morning, King Smelan, how are you? Are you enjoying your new dwelling? I'm on a short visit just to reassure you the day of the meeting with your family is round the corner. Everything is going according to plan. So while you enjoy seeing them and talking to them we will finish our job, the last stage of rejuvenating the people of these two continents. You will meet your family on the twentieth of December and make the speech on the twenty-fourth of December — Christmas Eve. How about this sequence, Your Majesty?"

"I think it's really good, logical and clear. OK, Nuri, go ahead, and you have my massive gratitude. My new family dwelling, the palace I should say, is beyond any dream! Any wall and any room reminds me, of who has built it. It is full of cutting-edge high tech and it will definitely help me and the family to catch up with reality. It is full of surprises, magical actions and motions in the house as if the house itself was alive, and had a personality. My Royal Gratitude to you Primleans! Whatever you do, you do it extraordinarily!"

Nuri started to glow and change colours — as you already know it was the Primleans' way to express joy and contentment. He sped away still aglow.

Now the king had a bit of time on his hands. He decided to organise his thoughts and step by step imagine the next days. They were so important, these last days of the greatest project Earth has ever had.

He contacted the committees of all continents again and told them that the celebrations on Earth would start on Christmas Eve, the twenty-fourth of December of the year 3999 and would last a week until New Year 4000 and several days after New Year. So they had to be totally ready for this great day and a splendid two week time of festivities afterwards.

He asked each continent to send to Eurasia some 'new' people to help with organising the festival on the Eurasia continent as they would not have much time before Christmas. He was assured by all committees that the people would be sent off to him and the continents would be ready for a flying start.

"Good, good," murmured the king. "Next, I have to polish the speech. Of course it is mostly ready and will be the same as I've done for other continents with the one important difference. That is that I shall have my family standing next to me and I shall have to tell the people about their revival. I shall do the preparation now," Smelan muttered to himself as he went to his little office. All the electronics were ready to be used — the satellite system, computer and hologram equipment.

Chapter 13

Smelan worked with inspiration, not noticing the hours flying by. He hardly had any coffee breaks. The king noticed that it was getting quite late only when the full smiley moon appeared in the dark starry sky.

"All right, I think I've done enough for today. I'd better have a good dinner looking at the beautiful stars. Now, I think I can imagine a bit better, just a tiny bit better, what is going on in space, all thanks to the astronomy course that Nuri introduced me to."

The king cooked dinner using tube food, which he didn't mind as the farmers were not yet producing crops. But this tube food was tasty and Smelan was used to it. He was eating slowly, dreamily looking at the stars, flying away in his thoughts to the sky. The stars were of different colours and sizes; they were twinkling, they were his friends or that's how he felt now. A deep peace relaxed his body and mind and he was in the mood to listen to some music.

He put on 'The Legend of the City of 'Kitezh' — the opera by Rimsky-Korsakov — music more than two thousand years old and still awakening one's imagination. A fascinating story, it tells that about two thousand, seven hundred years ago, a strong army of knights — all on horseback — conquered a vast country where a kind and peaceful people lived. These people had no army because they enjoyed life as it was; they were content and liked to laugh. When one likes to laugh there is no army needed.

In a faraway country there were a lot of angry people and they always wanted more of everything. How to get it? Ah, go to the neighbours and just take it — simple. So knights on horseback were riding across their neighbouring country like a wind, destroying and burning all the towns and villages. They wrecked the entire land and wiped out most of the population. They grabbed a lot of gold and stole the treasure of the country. It was a catastrophe; people who were still alive — only about twenty percent of them survived — were suffering hardship.

In the central part of the country, near the City of Kitezh, one duke was overlooked; he survived and started to call up people and gather the troops and soldiers to fight back against this furious and evil conqueror.

When the evil commander found out about this military gathering, he of course wanted to defeat them all. He ordered his warriors to ride towards the duke's army and annihilate them. The duke's army was a hundred times smaller and wouldn't be able to survive the battle. The duke knew that the enemy's army was superior, but he and his true friends — soldiers in arms — were not afraid of thousands and thousands of furious attackers.

They loved their native land, they did not want their people to be conquered and suffer. They prayed to God to help them withstand the enemy. The duke's soldiers stood like a rock waiting for the battle. They knew that they would die but they would die with honour for their native land.

It was the morning. The sun was rising and the bright sunshine was right in their eyes, blinding them, and the soldiers couldn't see the enemy army properly. So the duke had decided to relocate his soldiers when some of them started to notice that the frontmost galloping horses with warriors were somehow beginning to disappear: the front line, then the next line and the next. "what's going on?" — wondered the duke and his friends.

Shortly after, they started to hear a very low sound like a thunderstorm roaring as if it was not pleased with something. The ground had cracked open and this gap was getting wider and wider with every second. The enemy soldiers galloping up from behind didn't know about the gap; they couldn't stop suddenly, and in no time the whole army disappeared into this huge bottomless rupture.

The duke and his friends stared at it in disbelief. They prayed to God and praised him and thanked him. "To God, our savior," they sang, they whispered, they shouted being ecstatic, boundlessly grateful, and happy.

The next moment torrents of rain fell from the sky. The duke and soldiers were soaking wet but they couldn't move, as though enchanted. To say 'raining cats and dogs' was an understatement; it poured until the whole crack was filled with water. Then it stopped. A huge lake appeared right before their eyes. It was silent and peaceful all around. The sun was going down.

This legend has lived for about two thousand, seven hundred years and, who knows, maybe it is true? People who live near there say that from time to time they hear roaring thunder from the depths of the lake; people who go near the lake and wander in the forests do not come back. People say that some mysterious energy is present there and nobody knows what it is. Scientists have found plasma which frequently ignites. It is now like a ghost village — stunningly beautiful and scary.

Anyway the king liked this story and the opera. The music was like the story itself, all fantastic and mysterious. He wanted to listen to it especially now because it somehow echoed his own story, the story of Earth.

So Smelan set up the opera to listen to and enjoy. Music creates different emotions in the heart and different visions in the mind. This started to happen to the king exactly as if he was diving into the 'ocean' of music. The fantastic City of Kitezh was appearing as though from the clouds, clearer and clearer. Smelan started to make out details or maybe he was dreaming — he couldn't tell the difference now. At that moment he began to distinguish his wife, his daughter and behind them a crowd of their friends. The King rubbed his eyes but the group of people with his wife and daughter in front was really moving straight in his direction.

They stared at him. For a moment the king thought that he was losing his mind — the picture was so real and surreal at the same time. He closed his eyes quite tight thinking it would help him to shake off this mystical scenery. But when he opened his eyes his wife was sitting right next to him and his daughter was in the armchair opposite.

Smelan lost the power of speech and blacked out.

Chapter 14

A feeling that somebody was stroking his cheeks brought him back to the world. Still with eyes closed he recognised the gentle touch. Only one person in the world could caress him in this way — it was his wife. He was overwhelmed by this feeling and was afraid to open his eyes. He was not this afraid when he decided to fly to God to get help. But now... He started to breathe deeply without realising. Then, a tender kiss on both cheeks, then on the lips. "Lorella," he whispered, "it's you..."

"Yes, my darling," she breathed in his ear. The words of love and caring hurriedly followed. She asked him to open his eyes and meet all of them who had come to see him, to embrace him, to thank him. They were all so proud of him.

When the king opened his eyes, he saw a woman bending over him. She was not young and her hair was snow white. Her eyes glowed with love, piercing blue eyes he'd always adored. Of course it was his Lorella. She had changed a lot, so many years parted them, but his heart started beating as strongly and loudly as when he was twenty-five when they first met. "Lorella, now we shall never part again, never ever," said Smelan slowly. And they kissed and lay in each other's arms in a long, hug.

"Smelan, look now at your daughter and her children. You're a granddad now, Your Majesty. You have three grandchildren, one girl and two boys."

"But I don't see any girls and boys and where is my daughter?"

"My darling king, you have lost your mind from all this excitement. The children are growing so fast and in no time, they are adults, and they have their own children already. You have a big family now. Let me introduce all of them. Of course you recognise our sweet daughter, Yunona. And this is her husband, Yarosh, and here look, there are George and Peter. Yes, they don't look like small children anymore; you missed their childhood but now you can all catch up. Here is your youngest granddaughter, Bella; isn't she pretty? She looks very much like you when you were a child. I remember this photograph of you." Bella was looking at him with surprise and interest.

The king was lost; he felt his chest was too tiny in size for this tide of emotions. Lorella read it on his face and said, "You had such an important and dangerous mission, we're all very proud of you and happy to see you now — alive and really young! We're at the very beginning, starting our new wonderful life, thanks to you."

"My dearest, my beloved family, I suggest we start our new life today, right now. I know you'll have a million questions to ask and I have two million questions in return. But before we start talking, we shall now have a very good space-kind of lunch. I'll surprise you even more — I shall cook it on my own and it will be ready in fifteen to twenty minutes."

"You're boasting, my love. You can't cook a lunch for seven people in twenty minutes!"

"I can and I will. So now you can watch a bit of documentary programme while I am cooking." The king switched on the satellite system. Before going to the kitchen, he gave a kiss to each member of his family and, smiling broadly, disappeared.

All he had to do was go to a big fridge full of a selection of different types of tubes; there were no fewer than a hundred, of different tastes: small and bigger containers. He simply had to choose. He decided it would be good to start with a mushroom pâté on toast followed by a beautiful colourful beetroot soup. "Well, what would they like for the main course? Mm… let me guess, mm… mmm in the good old times we used to like trout or sea creatures. Ah, I have forgotten, my poor head; of course I have a lot of different seafood, for the sea hasn't been affected. What a joy, what a good idea!"

He went to the freezer and discovered a huge amount of different sea creatures. "Ah, dear Nuri, you're such a good boy, splendid idea, I see real treasure here."

The king chose seven starfish, one each, and intricately shaped seaweed. "Cooking time, five minutes, and ooh la la!" murmured the king. "Right now, what shall we have for dessert? Mmm, I think a gorgeous orangey and exotic buckthorn ice cream. Yes, I am pleased with my choice and now, turn and twist, dear Smelan," he said to himself. As he anticipated, in twenty minutes lunch was ready and the table laid to perfection.

It was a huge surprise for everybody that a king, a husband, and a father, and a grandfather managed to cook the whole lunch himself and in only twenty minutes. They were smiling and asked him how he had done it? The king answered with a smile that after his journey to the star, Prima, he had become a much more capable man, the first chef-King in history. "You know what?" he asked, "besides, I learned a lot about stars, and planets and space. Now I can even be a school teacher and the subject I'd teach would be astronomy. I totally fell in love with the eternal and everlasting universe. It's grandiose and it blows your mind. You want to explore it, to understand how it lives, how it interacts within. You want the universe to last forever! We have to keep an eye on it," smiled the king.

"Now, my dearest and beloved family, take your seats and I shall announce our first lunch on Earth together."

The table had an oval shape and a very strange surface on the top. There were no plates or cutlery. All the food — starters — was right on the table in the hollows in front of each person. Everybody looked at Smelan, and the king smiled, being very pleased with the effect of the Primleans' arrangement. He greeted all the family with a warm-hearted speech and told them just to think that they were ready to eat and then they would see what happened.

Then it was really fun; suddenly, in slightly different intervals of time, little portions of food floated straight to the mouth of each person at the table. Everybody was chewing the food at different speeds of course but there was no mess, it was a high-precision delivery of the portion to every mouth. The King saw round eyes full of surprise and delight. He was so happy to see these funny and happy faces.

When the starter was finished, miraculously all the plate-like hollows were cleaned and the king brought a big saucepan of beetroot soup.

The wonder continued; the invisible hand poured soup to everybody in their hollow. The same invisible style accompanied the whole lunch until all desserts were finished. All hollows were cleaned and then the top was flattened, no more hollows, flat as a pond in calm weather. "Wow, wow, how did it all happen?" said loud voices.

"Aha Primleans' miracle, magic."

The merry and excited family thanked the king for a delicious lunch with more fun than they'd ever had before.

"This is the beginning of a fun life on Earth now," said Smelan. "You will be surprised at what will be happening every day of your life."

What do you think, my friends, might be happening? You can discuss your ideas with your mates. Use your imagination — you like to fantasise, don't you?

Chapter 15

The king had taken the family to the garden, where most of the greenery has already been revived. It was a pleasant and not very hot afternoon. Everybody sat on the grass, they stroked it and one could see on their faces that they really enjoyed seeing it and touching it.

Smelan couldn't take his eyes off his wife and daughter but he just did not have time to stop and stare. So many things should be done before meeting the people and on top of this the time was coming up to Christmas. So he had to explain the situation to the family and added that they would be talking about everything — about life on Earth without the king and his travelling to God, and the Prima star. He wanted also to listen to the grandchildren and their fascinating stories of growing up. But! Big 'but' — time was pressing.

Everybody offered to help, and Smelan started to organise his family to give him a helping hand.

Next morning Nuri came bouncing in on his three legs. The king's family had just finished their breakfast and were sitting on the grass near the house. Smelan introduced Nuri to the family and told him that they were willing to help in any way they could.

Nuri was quick to think and in no time had come up with suggestions. He said that all the restoration work had been completed on this huge continent. "New people have been put in the new houses. I would suggest you try to make friends with them and see the difference between you and them. However, you might not notice any difference in perception of reality or the way they're thinking. The subject of history will help you to start communication. There are so many things for you to talk about — what has happened and what to expect in future. Then we'll meet again and you can tell me your observations. By the way, your experience might be helpful for the speech the king Smelan is going to make. Maybe he will decide to include these observations in the speech. And now I have to go, sorry — busy, busy. It was such a pleasure meeting you all personally. King Smelan told me a lot about you and I know how much he missed you, how much heartache he had when he travelled to Prima and back, and at each stage of his journey. I know this for sure because we can read minds. I'll see you soon," and he disappeared in an instant.

"What a nice Primlean," everybody said, "He's funny but very sweet and kind."

"Oh, I shall tell you so much about Nuri when we have a bit more time. Without him I probably would not have survived. He is a great man, I mean Primlean, I wanted to say, irreplaceable friend and a very, smart clever one."

Chapter 16

"Well, shall we follow Nuri's advice and take a jet to fly to our neighbours to make new friends," said the king.

Everybody jumped to their feet; everybody wanted to go. The king called for the jet and they watched the dragonfly-jet approaching fast. There could be seen great surprise and curiosity on faces. There was no pilot, but the king stepped inside and invited the others to join him. He looked like he knew what he was doing. Smelan went to the control board — click, click, click — and the engine started. In no time at all they saw a little town near a beautiful lake. The town looked unusual, strange new houses, all of slightly different sizes with gardens forming circles. In the middle of these circles were administrative buildings and a church.

The king landed outside the town and they as a group decided to go to the centre and find people there. They thought nobody would recognise this group of royal family as Royalty.

There were several cafes and a restaurant in the central square. The family had chosen one but when they approached it they saw an unusual setting inside. In the round hall, on the walls, there were big screen monitors each running a different programme. There were documentaries, music and cartoons for children. People looked focused on watching. All of them had ear-phones.

"What are we going to do?" the king asked the family. "It would be impolite to interrupt them. They look like they're not simply watching but learning."

"Shall we go to a restaurant then," suggested his wife. "We can find maybe some very unusual dishes and taste more Primlean food."

"What a splendid idea, off we go," and they started crossing the square when his grandson Peter saw two girls sitting on the edge of a fountain, chatting. Peter suggested inviting the girls to the restaurant and they could talk there.

"Goo-od thought," said Smelan enthusiastically. "Go, Peter, go, you're such a handsome young man, they will not refuse your invitation, believe me." With such encouragement Peter walked up to the girls.

"Sorry to interrupt you and, please, don't take this the wrong way but I am with my family here for the first time and we'd like to have lunch in this restaurant. Would you be so kind as to join us? We like your town and wanted to ask you about this place. Maybe we might move here. We'd like so much for you to spend some time with us." When the girls looked in the direction of the family, they nodded their heads and waved their arms.

"All right" said the girls, "it would be a pleasure for us to be your guides in this new place, we can tell you a lot about it."

"That is wonderful and so kind of you, thank you," and together they entered the restaurant.

The interior of the restaurant was astonishingly curious. One could see glowing tables with soft colours and above them under the high ceiling there appeared to be fluffy clouds. They provided the light, which was changing in the colours of the rainbow.

Do you know the rainbow colours, my friends, (memorised by English children in the mnemonic Richard Of York Gave Battle In Vain)?

They had chosen a table. It was a bit too small for such a large company, but just as they thought this, the table began to increase in size right before their eyes. Wow! The wonder started. Everybody looked at it with eyes wide open. Then a hologram appeared in the air, not far from them. A pleasant-looking young man greeted them and offered the menu.

The king nodded and smiled back at the waiter; they took their seats around the sparkling table. The girls introduced themselves, Ducy and Ann, and then it was the turn of the Royal family. The king looked at each member of the family and said simply, "I am King Smelan and this is my family."

The girls looked at each other and then jumped back from their seats. "Your Majesty," they said simultaneously in quiet voices. "Welcome back from your journey and thank you for what you have done for the Earth and its people. Yes, we heard on the news that there will be broadcasting this Saturday, Christmas Eve, and that you will tell the people more. We are learning from TV about this remarkable journey to the star Prima and we know that some Primleans are staying here with us. They helped a lot, in fact, they have returned life to the Earth, to the people."

"Yes, yes," nodded the king with a smile, "and now we will eat, drink, celebrate, and talk. Shall we choose our drinks and dishes? Look at that hologram menu; what would you like?"

There suddenly appeared the waiter, as a physical body, and said that just today the restaurant had a delivery of fresh natural eggs, fresh vegetables and fruit. Maybe you would like a real earthly lunch?" Everybody enthusiastically agreed it was a good idea apart from the youngest grandson, Peter. He wanted to have some dishes of space-food from tubes, and he ordered the selection with different tastes.

In no time their table became animated. The hollows had appeared in front of everybody and, as if by magic, pieces of aromatic omelette with vegetables filled them. Peter had a fancy configuration of bits smelling most exotic.

They ate with great appetite and talked about life on Earth during the king's absence. Smelan told them some travelling stories. The stories were mesmerising, absolutely fantastic, and difficult to believe. "You may have some doubts now, but when you see Primleans with your own eyes, it will convince you. It will be the day after tomorrow," said the king joyfully.

Chapter 17

It was dusk when they left the restaurant, and the girls expressed delight at seeing the Royal family and having lunch with them. Their eyes had a twinkle which was difficult to interpret — delight, surprise — yes, but still something not quite earthly, a riddle, and an enigma.

Next morning Nuri appeared after the family had had breakfast. As always, he curled his three legs in a compact way and placed himself in the armchair.

"So, Your Majesty, did you have a good evening yesterday? Have you got acquainted with anybody?"

"Yes, my dear friend. We had a lovely dinner in the evening in the town centre and we were not alone. Peter invited two young girls to have dinner with us and we talked and talked about many things. We found the girls were very smart, well-educated and very pleasant company. What we noticed — all of us — was a most mysterious look in their eyes. It has caused Peter to lose his night's sleep, hasn't it, Peter?" smiled the king.

"Well, it was some strange feeling about this glow in their eyes. I felt like it went right through me and left a feeling of some strange energy inside me. I've never felt like this before."

"Aha," said Nuri, "this modification comes from us, a little extra 'wiring' in the brainwaves of revived, reanimated people. Every time they look at you, they send you a little bit of positive energy, like a smile from head to head. I'm sorry to say it but they'll be more sensitive and have more power to transmit their senses to other people for better understanding. I told you before they'll be a bit different, more advanced, compared with the people who vanished during this disastrous attack. However, you yourself, and on behalf of all members of the Royal family, preferred to keep your DNA as it was before the attack. I think you are right in taking this decision; it will be good old Royal DNA and eventually you will mix with other people and it will give the strongest generation to come in the future."

"Wonderful," smiled the king and the others, "that's very interesting news and I think we have to expect now an eventful life, even more interesting than we experienced already. Thank you, Nuri, it's a great present to Earthlings."

"Dear Smelan, you have one more day to relax and on the evening of the twenty-fourth of December we'll have the celebrations started simultaneously over the whole Earth. Yes, I know your question; it will be Christmas Eve in Semper and different times on other continents — maybe morning, maybe night. But for the spirit of the celebration it doesn't matter, does it? Anyway, people can fly to Semper if they want to. Any kind of transport is available now."

"Before this, in the afternoon your speech will be transmitted to every corner of the Earth. You'll be surrounded by your family and maybe after the speech the people of the whole Earth will ask you questions about whatever they would like to find out. Do you think that's a good plan and will not be too tiring for you?"

"No, no, it sounds very good. So after my speech I will introduce the Primleans; do you think that's a good plan?"

"Yes, yes," said Nuri, "excellent. I'm going now but first I'll tell you that our Primlean surprise for the celebrations is still a little secret and we want it to be a surprise for you."

"I agree and I'm sure the surprise will be 'mind-blowing' indeed."

Chapter 18

Nuri had gone, and Smelan decided to contact all the celebration committees to tell them the time the celebration would start. All his family was helping him and by evening the job was done. "Excellent, and thank you very much, my darlings. I think today we'd better have dinner at home with 'prima food', because tomorrow will be a long and difficult day, the Greatest Day on Earth. We'd better go to bed early and have a good night's sleep."

So they cooked dinner together and ate it at their magically moving table. The king delayed going to bed, he wanted to reread his speech; read it to his wife to have her approval.

Next morning, the so long-awaited day had come: the twenty-fourth of December, 3999. Everybody got up very early; morning exercise, breakfast. Soon after they had finished Nuri appeared, all glowing with flickering, changing colours around his figure. It meant he was experiencing excitement.

"Good morning to you all. How do you feel this morning? I hope you are strong and ready for the Big Day. May I ask, Your Majesty, whether everything is at the launch stage?"

"Yes, dear Nuri, all preparations are complete. We can now jet to the communication centre for broadcasting. Just give us a little time to dress suitably for the occasion."

"Of course, Your Majesty, and meanwhile may I listen to some of your music? It will take me back to the historical romance period of Earth."

In half an hour everybody was dressed in Royal clothes for the occasion, ready to fly to the communication centre. It took them only twenty minutes to fly to Semper, the Earth's capital.

The spot where Semper had been built in the year 3000 would gratify even a sophisticated eye. It stood on a hill. Two picturesque winding rivers surrounded it from left and right. As far as the eye could see the smaller green hills circled around the 'mama' hill and become a bluish ribbon reaching to the horizon. The view had a hypnotic effect and when people stood there, right on the peak of the hill, they believed they could do everything they wanted; they had strength, and ability, and confidence. It was a magical place. A lot of people used to come here to put energy and spirit back in their lives, to recharge themselves.

The communication centre was situated in the central square and it took the group no more than five minutes to reach it. They saw that people had started to gather in the square and had to use the side door in order not to cause unnecessary excitement.

It was all ready for recording in the studio, and the only little thing remaining was to make up their faces; the king smiled but let it be done. The family took their seats around the king. Two broadcast reporters placed themselves to left and right in the family circle.

The clock struck eleven and the transmission began.

Chapter 19

All the people in the houses were glued to their TV or satellite system. There was a huge screen on the building in the square for people to watch. The king introduced himself and his family:

"I address you all, people of Earth, at home and on the square and wish to congratulate you on the ending forever of the suffering you have undergone. This catastrophe will never again strike Earth because we have been helped by the dwellers of the star Prima and they will provide the defence of Earth in the future.

"We celebrate the 'EARTH'S REVIVAL' and from now on we shall celebrate this remarkable event each year starting on Christmas Eve.

"I shall now introduce the heroes to you; they look very different from Earthlings and they are the kindest and most responsible dwellers of the Universe you could ever imagine."

Ay, Nuri, Ku, Lol and Staer had appeared on the screens. They looked different not only to Earthlings but to each other as well. Indeed, they were Aliens!

Nuri stepped forward and thanked the king for his introduction. He spoke in excellent English and said that it was impossible to tell the story in an hour about the king's journey to Prima but in the evening the people over the whole Earth would see a gigantic display in the sky. People of each continent could watch the 'sky film', which would play the whole night according to the time zone.

He continued: "My dear fellows of the Universe, my friends and colleagues from Prima were happy to be engaged in the Earth rejuvenation project. Our purpose in life is to keep the Universe going and support life on planets and stars where and when it is possible. We will always neutralise the dark forces of the Universe because their purpose is to eliminate life — any form of life. A small group of us are staying here doing some work on the orbital station. From time to time we could meet in Semper and do all sorts of things together. We like you, Earthlings. You are friendly and kind people, and more than this, you are curious, you like to learn about new things in life and in science. This is the best stimulus of progress leading you to ever-improving life."

Nuri stepped back and joined the group of Primleans, the constantly changing silhouettes of their bodies glowing with the constant change of colour. It was rather entertaining to watch.

Then the king spoke to the huge crowd of people about his journey, but not as much as he had planned as Nuri had told them now that everybody who wanted to know about the journey could watch the sky-high film. He announced that the dancing on the streets and sports would commence now, and after a lot of physical effort and to the fans' joy there would be a huge food delicatessen everywhere. It would be a real feast and people could enjoy as much as they want.

The orchestras started to play and people went in different directions both to play games and watch games. The music was heard in different parts of Semper as well the fans' loud voices.

Smelan turned to his family: "So the 'EARTH REVIVAL' celebrations have begun, my dears. What would you like to do?

"Shall we go and watch this ancient game of cricket? I always wanted to see the game but never had a chance." They all went to have a look at the cricket players.

However, what they saw was a far from traditional game. There were two teams of Primleans in the field and the speed at which they played cricket reminded them of a movie in fast-forward. All the members of the Royal Family looked at each other in astonishment. Their faces were perplexed. However, the crowd — mostly young people — responded to the game's movements without any delays as if it were a very ordinary game and players.

"In truth," thought the king to himself, "this is one of the differences of the 'new people' that Nuri talked about. It is interesting; what else, what other things are we going to see today?"

The king suggested taking an entertainment cab and going to watch a football match between Eurasia and South America. The cab was self-driving and there was a panel to manage the journey.

Smelan stepped to the panel and everybody heard a pleasant voice asking where they would like to go.

"We would like to watch a football match, if it's not too late."

"The football match has started already but there are a good fifty minutes left till the end of the game," said the cab.

"Good, we'll go there, please."

In no time the entertainment cab had delivered them to the stadium. The Royal family couldn't hide their surprise and delight. The speedy cab hardly touched the ground; sometimes when there were other vehicles on the road it just lifted itself in the air to overtake a car and then put itself down again on the road gently. "Wow, wow, father, I would like to have a car that can move like this cab," said Peter.

"We'll think about it, my dear boy. Now we, I hope, will enjoy the match."

They got to see two ordinary teams of players in differently glowing uniforms. They felt relieved. The speed of the running players was not over-excited and the glowing uniforms provided real entertainment. The king and family nostalgically enjoyed the game. Eurasia was winning and they were pleased. Smiling broadly, they were on their way out when the loud but pleasant voice announced that the shops, restaurants and cafés were open and invited everybody for the feast, gourmet meals and exquisite drinks — Primleans' magic drinks.

"Wow, it promises to be interesting; we definitely have to try the Primleans' drinks." They chose a random restaurant and joined a crowd of others. The name of the restaurant was the same as the name of the city, 'Semper'.

Chapter 20

There were a lot of people already, mostly young smiley faces. They looked excited. The Royalty chose a table, and from its position they could observe the hall of the restaurant and people. A waiter appeared from nowhere in a second. It was a young man dressed like an ancient Greek philosopher. They could read on his uniform 'From Plato to Semper'.

The first question to the waiter was of course not about menu or drink but about the wording on the uniform.

"What do you mean by having this wording, if I may ask?" said Peter. The waiter smiled and said it was just for educational purposes. If somebody was interested, they could just touch the words, and they would see a three-dimensional cloud in the air with all the information about this great man.

Other waiters had different names of famous people on their uniforms and it was a learning-with-fun idea.

"Indeed," said the king, "it's a splendid idea — knowledge through fun. Knowledge with a smile always sits better, more comfortably, in the head than knowledge by force.

"Well, now we would like to order our drinks and meal. Then we shall touch your magic logo and fly back in time to the great land of ancient Greece. I would like to add some words before we start our order. We are guests here from far away and we don't know much about the local food and drinks. So we shall put ourselves in your hands and would like to hear what you suggest."

"I'm honoured, Your Majesty! I am very pleased to meet your family as well and hope you all have a good time and an exquisite meal today. I cannot say that our restaurant is the best in the city — it would be looking down on others — but we are proud of our cuisine, our service, and our entertainment. I'm sure you'll enjoy it."

"Oh," said the king. "I was sure that people were so busy and excited now that nobody would notice the Royal family. It's really a pleasure talking to you, young man. Well, back to the menu. We would like to try the Primlean drink. We heard about it on the air."

"Yes, we have it but nobody has tried it yet. We do not know what kind of effect it will have. We're working and have to keep our heads clear and sound."

"Father, could we be the first to drink the Primlean's magic juices?" asked Peter, and George, and Bella with one voice.

"I think actually it should be me only. You see, I've lived my life and if something quite unexpected happened then it wouldn't matter so much. You are all young, you have life ahead and you have to be resilient, resourceful and with clear strong minds."

"My dear Smelan," exclaimed his wife. "What about me? I want to be with you whatever happens. Shall we drink the juice together and the children will follow us. I am sure we will all be fine but if you, Your Majesty, insist on being the first, then so be it."

"Right, a compromise is found. Good for us."

Now the king turned to the waiter and asked him to bring the drinks.

"Which one would you like?" asked the waiter.

"Do you have different tasting drinks or different colours?"

"Yes, we have both, different taste and different coloured drinks, but also with different effects following. Here is the menu of the 'miracles' one can expect."

The eyes on all faces widened and rounded. Peter, George and Bella could hardly keep still on their seats.

"Father, please read it out loud, it's incredibly interesting."

"Yes, my children, what a surprise the Primleans have in their sophisticated minds. I am intrigued myself and feel impatient like you, my precious."

"Well, well, it's a whole page to read. Will you please excuse us?" He turned to the waiter. "It will take a bit of time to make a decision with such an unusual 'menu'."

"Of course, Your Majesty, I understand this. I shall be back when you're ready. Just raise your finger and I shall see you on our service screen. Good luck and take your time." The waiter had gone, and the family prepared to be 'all ears'.

Chapter 21

"Are you ready, my dears! Right, here are five magical drinks, all of them with the effect of virtual reality:

"First — feeling as though you are an astronaut on board the spaceship.

"Second — feeling as though you are on a trip around the star Prima.

"Third — feeling you're communicating with Primleans and you understand each other.

"Fourth — you are on a tour around the Earth observing the disaster that happened.

"Fifth — you are on a tour around the Earth looking at the future of mankind on Earth."

"There we are. Any ideas, any preferences?"

The boys, Peter and George, were of course the first to spring up with a choice. They wanted to have an experience of the astronauts; then Bella joined them. Their daughter, Yunona, was of a quiet personality and she chose the excursion around the Earth to see what the future held. However, her husband, Yarosh, decided to learn about the horror on the Earth in the past. He was a history teacher, and it was a professional interest for him. The King himself chose the excursion around the star Prima. He advised his wife, Lorella, to be with him on this excursion and choose the same drink. She agreed of course to follow her beloved husband. So all choices were made and the king raised his finger.

The waiter appeared immediately as promised and took all the orders, and soon he appeared with the tray of drinks. The glasses were of an unusual shape and texture. Actually, they changed their shape all the time as if they were alive. But, most intriguing and maybe even scary, were the drinks themselves. Some of them were steaming with sparkling liquid running out of the glass; the others looked as if the liquid was boiling although the wriggling glass was cold. Yarosh's glass was absolutely black with loudly hissing liquid streaming down the glass, grumbling, and evaporating on its way.

Everybody was astounded looking at their glasses; they were not brave enough to have a first sip. They wanted to ask the waiter but he had evaporated too. Then the king said, "So my lovely, shall we be brave? Our adventure starts right now, right here! I'm sure the Primleans wish us all well and it's just their practical joke to make our blood run faster and hearts beat louder. Cheers everybody!"

Chapter 22

The king drank his twisting glass and put it on the table; the glass stopped twisting and became a quite ordinary insignificant object. The others carefully took their glasses, sniffing and looking inside.

The next brave ones were the boys; they followed their father's approach and quickly drank the liquid. One after another, they drank their peculiar 'live' juices. Bella followed her brothers and said that the juice was deliciously-strange.

By this time the restaurant was full of people behaving in entertaining ways. They were in a role play but did not realise it; some of them were giving instructions to someone who was supposed to be next to them but there was nobody... Some of them were sitting with faces full of surprise or delight. It's really difficult to describe all the variety of behaviour but it definitely was great fun for the waiters to watch their customers as everybody who came to the restaurant wanted to have this magical Primlean drink. The whole atmosphere was fantastic beyond words, nutty as a fruitcake...

Half an hour passed and the royal family one by one started to come back to reality. Their faces still reflected recently-lived emotions; they couldn't speak and took time to come to their senses. After a while Smelan exclaimed, "Well, my dears, I am very glad to see you are still here, and not in the spaceship or fifty years back in time on Earth or maybe a hundred years in the future. I think it will take us a long time to tell each other head-spinning stories. Ye-ees, the Primleans certainly surprised us all indeed. They will be pleased to hear that we were all bewildered and shocked, in a good way of course. A-ah, dear Primleans, I like you, I love you, despite that we don't really know how you look. You are elusive and keep changing all the time. Yet, you are the most intellectual and astonishing Primakind in the universe.

"I hope humankind had the same potential ability in the future. Well, what shall we eat now after such exciting drinks?"

Out of nowhere the waiter appeared. He pointed his finger up and the menu hung in the air in front of them. There were two major selections of food: one selection was all freshly grown food on Earth, and the other was the Primleans' fantasy. The choice was unusual and tantalising. At this moment they all wanted to forget about modesty and choose not just one or two dishes, but this and that and those...

Smelan looked at his family and a sparkle appeared in his eyes. "I have a suggestion, my dearest, what if we take whatever we want and put everything on the table? Then each of us can try a bit. We shall have a selection of everything. I have to allow you to be so curiously greedy this once as it is a special occasion. Only one time — never ever again. It is bad, bad for you my dearest," he smiled.

Smelan glanced at the waiter and told him that they were going to have a truly king's feast. The Royal family would like to try everything; therefore they'd order all the existing menu dishes. The waiter smiled and said that it was a truly perfect choice.

They started to share their stories with each other while waiting for the promised feast.

It did not take long to be astonished at the three-tiered trolley appearing in front of their table. The dishes lifted themselves from the trolley, moved towards the table, and found their place on it. In no time and without any effort from the waiter the table was laid beautifully with unusual-coloured dishes which filled the nostrils with tantalising smells. Nobody could say a word as it was all a sudden amusement to watch.

Smelan stood up and said only one sentence: "Enjoy the present of the Primleans; their imagination and ingenuity have no bounds; it all looks fantastically alien, but I hope it's all edible. Forward, my dears."

Smelan sat down and just as he wanted to reach for something this little red-purple piece arrived at his mouth and he had to open it as the morsel squeaked 'mmm-eee'. Everybody stared at the king as if he had just swallowed a froggie.

"Good Lord, was that tasty!" exclaimed Smelan. "I don't know what it was but it tasted heavenly. Be brave; go ahead, the Primleans want to surprise us, to amuse us. Maybe it is their only chance because they will return to the star Prima (most of them anyway.)"

However even after reassurance the members of the Royal family did not rush to have something. It was not surprising though. Apart from the earthly food which looked familiar and very inviting, the other, so-to-speak, 'food', looked hardly edible but much more entertaining. The colour of different pieces on the plates kept changing and pieces themselves kept moving — either circling in the big dish or jumping from one plate to another. More than this they made different sounds like a small ha-ha-ha, or heee-yy, or mm-vaa. It was such fun to watch all of them. Nobody knew how it would be possible to eat these jolly and friendly pieces of food.

Then the king, who was familiar with the tricks of Primleans, advised them just to think what they would like to try and see what happened. Everybody followed his advice and suddenly the food on the dishes started to move in all directions. It was flying and jumping from the plates right to the mouths of all guests. Everybody was smiling, laughing, chewing and clearly enjoying the Primleans' surprise. The flying and dancing yummy pieces of food astounded everybody.

The royalty were in great spirits as if the dancing food filled them with cheer and good energy. Their eyes were glowing with jollity. The King saw this and was very pleased to feel that all his family was in such good form and happy.

They thanked the waiter and invited him to visit them in their dwelling. "It was unique food, a unique meal and atmosphere. We were bewitched by this place and will definitely come here again." The waiter was glad to be invited and added that this day was a very special day and that food like this was served that day (and would last the whole week) at any restaurant on Earth. It was the Primleans' arrangement, the gift from them to all Earthlings. He smiled. "Now I say goodbye and will see you later in the New Year."

The Royal family left the restaurant.

Chapter 23

Out in the square they saw a crowd, and everyone was looking at the sky. The sky turned out to be 'the all sky performance'. Bewildered royalty had to get their bearings to stay on their feet. As far as the horizon they could see different movies of different stages of the king travelling. They could see the star Prima and the future of Earth — all blooming beautiful land with people, smiling, dancing, playing music, and working. They noticed they had contented faces with no anger on them. 'Happy days' one could say.

Suddenly Nuri appeared. His 'stony'-like face was not stony now at all. He was smiling too like a human being!

"Nuri," exclaimed Smelan, "you're smiling!" The King was less surprised at Nuri's appearance than his broad smile. "Yes, Your Majesty, you know I am a good student, so I have learned how to smile, and it gives me a great deal of pleasure. I really like this exercise and the feelings attached to it. I would like to introduce this earthly ancient innovation to all Primleans. It will be your gift — from Earthlings to Primleans."

"What a good idea, Nuri, you do it. And let me now express the boundless gratitude for an amazing, bewitching celebration party. It is really head-spinning. Everywhere you go, you see unearthly surprise and your fantasy paid off overwhelmingly!" Nuri smiled again broadly. One could notice that he enjoyed doing it. "How did you do all this and on such a scale!" The King couldn't stop himself asking questions.

"Dear King Smelan, you will understand it in about one million years, but maybe a bit earlier when your civilisation reaches the level we are at now."

"The EARTH REVIVAL celebrations over the whole Earth will last until New Year and then two or three days after. Then Primleans will say their goodbyes and leave. You know several of us will stay in the orbital station and visit you from time to time to practise smiling," grinned Nuri again. "I want to tell you one more thing — you will get another surprise on New Year's Eve before the Primleans leave. Now I have to fly because I am in charge of many things and want to be sure that everything is going smoothly in the Primlean way, meaning perfect." Nuri jetted out in the air.

"What could it be?" the intrigued Royalty asked each other. "We shall wait and see," said the king. "You can never guess what and how their fantasy and technology will play with our minds. They are the masters of miracle-making. Now we can enjoy the magnificent sky. Look, look, you see this iridescent cloud, it's me talking to God, and there's the spaceship; and me in a protective astronaut suit. I see it for the first time; I couldn't see myself of course when I was in this suit."

There were a lot of people in the square with their heads looking up at the sky. The magical display stretched as far as the eye could see. It was fascinating, impressive and hardly believable that what they saw actually was reality in the recent past. Nobody wanted to leave the square; one could hear excited voices and uplifted arms drawing something in the air.

Exactly at midnight the display started to fade and before it was gone the message appeared that it would be rolling the whole week until New Year. Natural night sky with stars embraced the Earth.

The King and family went home all affected by the remarkable vision. Then Smelan said, "Tomorrow is Christmas. I suggest we have a quiet time this year. There is much to talk about and we can enjoy each other's company. What if we go to church in the morning and then stay at home and in the garden, trying to adjust to the new era, a new life? We definitely need a break to plant our feet firmly on the ground."

"Yes, that is sensible indeed," added Lorella. "It will be good to have time together at long last.

Chapter 24

The next days were relatively quiet. After church and a beautiful Christmas service, the Royal family spent time together at home. They cooked Christmas lunch themselves because it was fun to cook the 'flying' food; then they were eating the unusual meal off flying plates. There were eyes, round from astonishment again, and laughter because sometimes the plates seemed to be confused, and some people would have two portions of dessert and others none. Mainly the children had several portions of dessert, and Smelan and Lorella were passed by. "What confusingly clever plates," murmured Smelan with a grin.

After lunch the family decided that there was no time for a rest despite the Christmas festivities. They needed to catch up with the novelty of the new life of learning extraordinary skills. Primleans introduced advanced technology and ways of communication in all different aspects of ordinary life. The King and Lorella were struggling to grasp the super complexity and the speed of the life changes. Fortunately, their children and grandchildren were soaking up all innovations and felt thrilled at diving into unknown modernity.

The young people had discovered a new ability within themselves — their bodies were able to do quite tricky gymnastic moves and their minds were powerful enough to send a wish which could become a reality. Wow!

"Life appears to be rather different now," murmured Smelan to himself, when he saw youngsters in the streets jumping higher than kangaroos or somebody crossing a square doing somersaults. "Well, well, it is all very interesting; what will be the next surprise?" thought the king. "I cannot guess; Primleans are beyond all imagination."

It seemed to Smelan that the moment he touched the ground on the Earth was only yesterday. Now, after all the curious events and Primleans' performances and interaction, the time appeared to be passing with the speed of light.

"It is New Year in two days. I haven't seen Nuri for ages... where is he? What is he doing? Actually, I don't even know his gender — maybe he is 'she'. In fact, it is totally unknown to me who is who," thought the king for the first time. "However, I don't feel comfortable asking about it; maybe it's a sensitive matter? Hmm.

"Anyway, I would be really happy to see Nuri today," and he knew that Nuri would come as he would receive the message in space.

Nuri appeared quite soon indeed.

The king grinned and opened his arms to give Nuri a hug. It was not easy however to embrace the stony star-shaped figure of Nuri.

"Yes, yes, I know you love me, dear Smelan," he said in a sweet, now female-sounding voice. I wouldn't mind having a flying cup of coffee." He sat in his favourite armchair.

"One moment, my dear Nuri, of course. Why did you say 'flying'?"

"Because it is flying," chuckled Nuri. The king saw his travel cup with aromatic coffee almost by his lips. Another cup was 'floating' towards Nuri. "Here we are, King Smelan, Merry Christmas to you and your family!" One of the hands of the star-legged Nuri sucked the coffee in. It made a 'bulle-bulle' sound when flashing down the silhouette. "Hmmm," mumbled Smelan, "most unusual sound when one eats."

"It's kind of an earthly miracle", continued Nuri. "I am used to drinking coffee now and you know what? I don't have 'indigestion', I enjoy it. I've discovered that coffee made me glow brighter"

"It's an earthly miracle indeed and I'm glad to learn that you've found such an innovative application for coffee. I must tell my family about this curiosity, ha-ha."

"Your Majesty, I can tell you another little secret that we Primleans learned here. Would you like to know it now?"

"If it's a secret then I would prefer to be stunned — pleasantly of course — when the time comes."

"You are right, Your Majesty; a secret is sweeter when one can wait to discover it. However, I shall at least tell you the time so your family will not miss it."

"All right, Nuri, when is your surprise visiting time?"

"It is New Year's Eve. You go outside and look at the sky. I'll say no more."

"Nuri, we look at the sky every day to watch this striking travel story. We're never tired of it for we're discovering more and more interesting and beautiful details. You show it differently each day."

"King Smelan, it will be a peculiar display. Not a word of explanation. I will see you and the family on New Year's Eve."

"Uh-oh, a 'flying cup' of coffee was perfect for a 'stony' stomach," giggled Nuri. "Thank you, King Smelan. Please, pass my Christmas greeting to your lovely family; you are a happy man to have such good kin."

As always Nuri disappeared in a moment.

"Hmm, what is it?" thought the king. "Ah, there's no way to guess, I cannot outwit the masters of miracles."

Chapter 25

That special moment had somehow come on suddenly. Life now was engaging, stimulating and intensive, packed with unusual activities both mental and physical. Therefore, nobody was watching the clock ticking. All members of the family slept for about five hours and it was enough — nobody felt tired or dragging their feet from lack of rest.

The first who suddenly saw it before the king was his grandson, George. He literally jumped into the house and yelled, "Quick, quick, everybody out now! It's the funniest thing I've ever seen! Honestly you will die laughing!"

Everybody dropped whatever they were doing and dashed outside. As George predicted one could see surprised, stunned faces with mouths gaping; perhaps one could say 'jaw-dropping' faces.

Wow, what was happening in the sky was difficult to describe without at least a grin. One definitely had to have no sense of humour at all to keep a straight face.

The Primleans were dancing, not just rock 'n' roll or samba-like. It was ballet dancing in costumes to show the characters of different personages. However, their 'arms', 'legs' and other parts of their unearthly silhouettes were in a dramatically funny dissonance to mankind's classic appearance on the stage.

"We shouldn't really giggle," said the king. That was another surprise Nuri mentioned before. They learned how to dance and they did it beautifully, in costumes, to surprise people and give a wonderful performance. "They are what they are. Even we, people, are all different and sure we don't mind a different body shape or unconventional appearance. The Primleans are from a different galaxy; of course all the intellectual creatures of the universe are evolving in a variety of natural conditions that one cannot ever imagine. Shall we enjoy this beautiful 'food for the soul' performance? As for me, I admire their creativity — look, all the costumes are well fitted and they have such colourful wraps too. Music is performed with perfection; one cannot fault them.'

"Oh, look," Peter called, "some of their real images start disappearing and instead one can see the configurations of different lights."

"It is getting darker and they thought about us; they know we cannot see at night. So they have come up with this idea of performing (be it opera or ballet or anything else) with dancing and changing lights. It is so beautiful, isn't it? And the characters are so real and clear to feel and understand. How can they do it?"

"I think," Peter said, "they are sending us a mental script of each character and we are receiving their signals together with the light images, so that we have the whole picture of what's going on in the sky."

"Peter, it sounds credible," said Yarosh. "I agree with you. Well done, son."

The performance in the sky lasted the whole night, with the break for New Year 4000.

From nine p.m. of the year 3999 till three a.m. in the morning of New Year 4000 the Primleans put on display the celebrations in all the continents and countries.

If one could see Earth from space they would be surprised to watch the planet fluctuating and flickering with different beams of light and humming with music.

Chapter 26

So, the Year 4000, a happy year, a New Start year, the New Life on Earth year has come!

And you, my friends, can use your imagination and draw the pictures of this celebration and make up some stories of this festive time. It will be great fun.

The Primleans were staying one more week. They are leaving on the seventh of January at midnight to make their departure beautiful with illuminations. People from many towns of different continents have come to Semper to express their deep gratitude and say goodbye to such kind, mesmerising intellectuals who have become their friends.

They are leaving Earthlings some gifts: the memorable display of the king's journey; also, all recordings of the Primleans' deeds after landing on Earth; King Smelan's speeches and the celebration of the unforgettable Christmas and historic New Year 4000.

The seventh of January, year 4000, midnight.

"Without a doubt the Earthlings will never forget the extraordinary Primleans," King Smelan started his speech, their generosity, their way of living life, of lending a helping hand, whether it is to close friends or faraway neighbours in the Universe. The Primleans showed us what we can achieve in science, how we can progress in our minds. Their boundless creativity, which they enjoy every moment in their long lives makes them jolly, happy individuals. We have to remember this message — we could be them in several centuries," so the king ended speaking.

They were the last words of a short King's speech. It was already dark night in Semper. Millions of people gathered to get out and watch the departure of the Primleans' starships. Smelan was sad and could barely hide his emotions. He was attached to these sweet, modest, ever kindly creatures. Suddenly Nuri appeared next to the king.

"Dear Smelan, you are the king... I know what you feel, I can read your mind, but you know it is a part of life — meeting and parting. Of course you know this.

"What about having your travel 'flying' cup of coffee? Or maybe champagne would be better on this occasion?"

"Nuri, you always make me smile. Yes, dear friend, sure I would like to have now my travelling 'flying' cup of coffee. It reminds me the first time I met you, and then..."

"That is such a good answer. Ahh... here we are."

The King sniffed the beautiful aroma of Nuri's coffee and had a sip.

Suddenly the dark sky enraptured them. Hundreds of different-coloured beams of light started to trace the sky. They were spinning and making fanciful geometric traces and in time one by one fading in the darkness of space.

The Primleans had turned the page; they were going on a different mission now. They were destined to search for a new home.

"Good bye, my dearest friends," the king whispered, unable to hide his emotions any longer.

He has been surrounded by his family in the midst of thousands and thousands of 'new people'.

Chapter 27

Never forget how to laugh!

Post Scriptum

New towns have appeared in the kingdom and their names are:

Nuri
Ay
Staer
Lol
Ku

Characters

Smelan	the King of the Earth
Yunona	daughter of the king
Lorella	wife of the king
Yarosh	husband of Yunona
Peter	the king's grandson
George	the king's grandson
Bella	the king's granddaughter
Nuri	Primlean, coordinator
Ku	Primlean, chairman of the Committee
Ay	Primlean, captain of the Interstellar ship
Issa	Primlean, responsible for landscaping
Lol	Primlean, scientist
Staer	Primlean, astrophysicist
Hier	Primlean, scientist
Zoom	Primlean, scientist
Primleans/ Superbiotechs	Inhabitants of Prima
Antipodals	evil inhabitants from an enemy galaxy

IS	Interstellar ship
CSE	Committee for the Salvation of Earth
Tugri	money
Semper	town/city, in Latin means 'forever'!